爱　经

The Art of Love

[古罗马] 奥维德　著

戴望舒　译

时代文艺出版社

图书在版编目（CIP）数据

爱经 / (古罗马) 奥维德 著；戴望舒 译. —长春：时代文艺出版社，2012.12（2021.5重印）

ISBN 978-7-5387-3698-4

I. ①爱... II. ①奥...②戴... III. ①爱情诗 – 诗集 – 古罗马 IV. ①I546.22

中国版本图书馆CIP数据核字（2012）第266874号

出品人 陈琛

责任编辑 付 娜

装帧设计 孙 俪

排版制作 隋淑凤

爱 经

[古罗马] 奥维德 著　戴望舒 译

出版发行 / 时代文艺出版社

地址 / 长春市福祉大路5788号　龙腾国际大厦A座15层　邮编 / 130118

总编办 / 0431-81629751　发行部 / 0431-81629755

官方微博 / weibo.com / tlapress　天猫旗舰店 / sdwycbsgf.tmall.com

印刷 / 保定市铭泰达印刷有限公司

开本 / 640×980毫米　1 / 20　字数 / 148千字　印张 / 13

版次 / 2013年3月第1版　印次 / 2021年5月第2次印刷　定价 / 39.80元

图书如有印装错误　请寄回印厂调换

出　版　说　明

　　本书是古罗马著名诗人奥维德创作的长诗"*Ars Amatoria*"，英译名为"*The Art of Love*"，翻译为《爱的艺术》，戴望舒译为《爱经》。这是一部描写爱的技巧，传授男女恋爱之术的两性爱情宝典，是古罗马"镀金时代"的爱情大师奥维德专为世间恋人谱写的爱情教科书。

　　本书分为三卷，奥维德假称受爱神和爱神之母委托，分别向男女两性宣讲恋爱的技巧和艺术。第一卷旨在告诉男人如何获得爱情；第二卷是要告诉男人如何保持爱情；第三卷则告诉女人如何追求爱情。其中，第一卷向男性宣讲恋爱的场所，教导男性应该到何处去寻找自己喜爱的女子以及怎样接近并取悦她们的艺术；第二卷继续向男性说法，指导他们应当如何维系与所爱女子的爱情关系；第三卷是女性的课堂，鼓励女性要积极主动地对待爱情，教导女性如何取悦男人、如何使爱情久长的艺术。

　　此书历来被认为是古罗马文学史上一部十分独特的书，是一部大胆绮靡的文学经典，一部命运多舛的旷世奇书。它既被斥为坏书，又被誉为天才的著作。由于书的内容惊世骇俗，是以传授男女爱情之术为主旨，这与奥古斯都推行的道德改革政策发生冲突，所以公元8年诗人被流放，十年之后忧郁而亡。这本书在历史上也屡次被禁，开了世界禁书的先河。

因为是禁书，原为古拉丁文的《爱经》流传下来的古抄本极少。英国牛津、奥地利维也纳、法国巴黎各仅存一套，最为完备者当属法国巴黎本，所以近代几种主要欧洲文字的译本都是根据巴黎本译出。国内第一个翻译此书的戴望舒也是从巴黎本译出的，1929年由上海水沫书店初版，改书名为《爱经》。戴望舒虽然将原诗译成散文，却保留着原作的诗意，语言精雕细琢、委婉细腻，给人以唯美的艺术享受。所附的英文版是詹姆斯·刘易斯·梅于1929年翻译的，她从古拉丁语翻译成英文同戴望舒从法语翻译成中文的时间很接近，对原作品的理解也比较一致，所以选择此译本。

《爱经》通篇洋溢着文学的诗情画意和情爱的浪漫气息，引用了大量希腊、罗马神话中的爱情故事，所以编者搜集了大量有关古希腊和罗马神话的图片，以增加读者的阅读兴趣并给读者直观的美的视觉和精神享受。另外，原中译本中有很多民国时期的翻译人名和地名，与现代译法不尽相同，我们都尽力予以校正，以便读者能更好地阅读和理解此书。

译 者 序

奥维德（Publius Ovidius Naso）于公元前43年生于苏尔摩。与贺拉斯、卡图鲁斯及维吉尔并称为罗马四大诗人。奥维德髫龄即善吟咏，方其负笈罗马学律时，即以诗集《恋歌》为世瞩目。渐乃刻意为诗，秾艳瑰丽，开香奁诗之宗派，加都路思之后，一人而已。

至其生平，无足著录，惟曾流戍玄海之滨，此则为其一生之大关键，《黑海零简》及《哀歌》，即成于此。盖幽凉寂寞之生涯。实有助于诗情之要渺也。惟其流戍之由，亦莫能详，或谓其曾与奥古斯都大帝孙女茹丽亚有所爱恋，遂于帝怒，致蒙斥逐，顾无可征信，存疑而已。要之以作者之才华，处淫靡之时代，醇酒妇人，以送华年，殆至白发飘零，遂多百感苍凉之叹，亦固其所耳。

奥维德著述甚富，有《爱经》《爱药》《岁时记》《变形记》

《哀歌》等各若干卷，均为古典文学之精髓。今兹所译《爱经》（*Ars Amatoria*）三卷，尤有名。前二卷成于公元前1年，第三卷则问世稍后，然皆当其意气轩昂，风流飙举之时。以缤纷之辞藻，抒仕女容悦之术，于恋爱心理，阐发无遗，而其引用古代神话故事，尤见渊博，故虽遣意狎亵，而无伤于典雅；读其书者，为之色飞魂动，而不陷于淫佚。文字之功，一至于此，吁，可赞矣！奥氏晚岁颇悔其少作，而于《爱经》，犹自悔艾，因作《爱药》，以为盖愆。顾和凝《红叶》之集，羡门《延露》之词，均以晚年收毁而愈为世珍；古今中外，如出一辙也。

诗不能译，而古诗尤不能译。然译者于此书。固甚珍视，遂发愿以散文译之，但求达情而已。至所据版本，则为亨利·鲍尔奈克（Henri Bornecque）教授纂定本，盖依巴黎图书馆藏10世纪抄本，及牛津图书馆藏9世纪抄本所校订者也。

目　录
CONTENTS

第一卷

如何获得爱情

Finding Love

假如在我们国人中有人不懂得爱术，他只要读了这篇诗，读时他便理会，他便会爱了。

　　用帆和桨使船儿航行得很快的是艺术，使车儿驰行得很轻捷的是艺术；艺术亦应得统治丘比特。奥托墨冬①善于驾车和运用那柔顺的马缰；提费斯②是海蒙尼亚船③的舵工。而我呢，维纳斯曾经叫我做过她的小丘比特的老师，人们将称我为丘比特的提费斯和奥托墨冬。他是生来倔强的，他时常向我顽抗，但是他是个孩

■ 维纳斯与丘比特　布歇

①阿喀琉斯的御者。
②伊阿宋取金羊毛所乘阿尔戈船的舵手。
③指阿尔戈船。以珀利翁山上的树木制成。山在忒沙利亚，忒沙利亚旧名海蒙尼亚，故名。

子，柔顺的年龄，是听人指挥的。菲丽拉的儿子①用琴韵来教育阿喀琉斯，靠这平寂的艺术，驯服了他的野性。这个人，他多少次使他的同伴和他的敌人恐怖。有人说看见他在一个衰颓的老人前却战栗着；他的那双使赫克托耳②都感到分量的手，当老师叫他拿出来时，他却会伸出来受罚。

喀戎是埃阿科斯③的孙子的蒙师；我呢，我是丘比特的。两个都是可畏的孩子，两个都是女神的儿子。可是骄恣的雄牛终究驾着耕犁之轭，勇敢的战马徒然嚼着那控制着它的辔头。我亦如此。我降伏丘比特④，虽然他的箭伤了我的心，又在我面前摇动着他的明耀的火炬。他的箭愈是尖，他的火愈是烈，他愈是激起我去报复我的伤痕。

阿波罗⑤啊，我绝不会冒充说我所教的艺术是受你的影响而来的；传授我这艺术的更不是鸟儿的歌声和振羽；当我在你的山谷阿斯克拉⑥牧羊时，我没有看见过克利俄⑦和克利俄的姐妹们。

---

①半人半马的喀戎，菲丽拉为其母。
②特洛伊战争中的大将，后为阿喀琉斯杀死。
③阿喀琉斯的祖父。
④维纳斯的儿子，有一副能唤起人们爱欲的神箭。
⑤太阳神，也是文艺之神。
⑥古希腊大诗人赫西奥德的故乡。
⑦九位缪斯之一，司历史。

■ 维纳斯的胜利 布歇

——轻盈的细带是贞洁的象征，维纳斯的带子，既象征一种绝对的诱惑，也表示贞操的丧失。

经验是我的导师：听从有心得的诗人吧。真实，这就是我要唱的："帮助我吧，丘比特的母亲！走开得远些，你轻盈的细带①，贞节的表征；而你，曳地的长衣，你将我们的贵妇们的纤足遮住了一半！我们要唱的是没有危险的欢乐和被批准的偷香窃玉，我的诗是没有一点可以责备的。

———————————

①指维纳斯腰间的带子，只有待字闺中的女子可以佩带，但奴隶和外国人即使未嫁也无权佩带。

愿意投到维纳斯①旗帜下的学习兵，第一，你当留心去寻找你的恋爱的对象；第二，你当留心去吸引那你所心爱的女子；第三，要使这爱情维持久长。这就是我的范围；这就是我的马车要跑的跑场，这就是那应当达到的目的。

当你一无羁绊，任意地要到哪里就到哪里的时光，你去选一个可以向她说"唯有你使我怜爱"的人儿。她不会乘着一阵好风从天上吹下来的，那中你的意的美人是应当用你的眼睛去找的。猎人很知道他应该在什么地方张他的鹿网，他很知道在哪一个谷中有野猪的巢穴。捕鸟的人认识哪儿是利于他的黏竿的树林，而渔夫也不会不知道在哪一条水中鱼最多。你也如此，要找一个经久的爱情的目的物，亦应该第一个知道在哪里能遇着许多少女。

要去找她们，你也用不着坐船航海，也用不着旅行到远方去。珀耳修斯②从熏黑的印度人中找到他的安德洛墨达③；弗里吉亚人④掠到了一个希腊女子。我很愿意这样。但是单单一个罗马

---

① 爱情女神，司性爱与美貌。
② 希腊英雄，主神宙斯化作金雨与达那厄发生关系所生之子。
③ 埃塞俄比亚公主，珀耳修斯之妻。
④ 指特洛伊王子帕里斯，诱拐斯巴达王后海伦导致特洛伊战争。希腊女子即指美女海伦。

已够供给你一样美丽的女子，又如此的多，使你不得不承认说："我们的城中有世界一切的美人。"正如迦尔迦拉之丰于麦穗，麦提姆那之富有葡萄，海洋之有鱼，树林之有鸟，天空之有星，在你所居住着的罗马，也一样地有如此许多的年轻的美女。丘比特的母亲已在她亲爱的埃涅阿斯①的城中定了居所。假如你是迷恋着青春年少又正在发育的美女，一个真正无瑕的少女就会使你看中意了；假如你喜欢年纪大一点的，成千的少妇都会使你欢心，而你便会有选择的困难了。可是或许一个中年有经验的妇人在你是格外有情趣，那么，相信我，这种人更多了。

当太阳触到海尔古赖斯的狮子背脊的时候②，你只要到庞培③门的凉荫下慢慢地去散步，或是在那个慈母为要加一重礼物到她儿子的礼物上，使人用异国的云石造成的华丽的纪念物④旁闲行。不要忘记去访问那充满了古书的廊庑，名叫利维亚，这也就是它的创立者的名字。也不要忘了你在那里可以看见那些谋害不幸

---

①罗马始祖，维纳斯的儿子。
②指七月。
③庞培（公元前107—前48），罗马大将。
④指屋大维门和马尔凯卢斯剧场，马尔凯卢斯是屋大维的儿子。

的堂兄弟们的培鲁斯的孙女们①和她们的手中握着剑的残忍的父亲的廊庑。更不要忘记那维纳斯所哀哭的阿多尼斯节②，和叙利亚的犹太人每礼拜第七日所举行的大祭典。更不要用避开母牛，埃及的披着麻衣的女神③的神殿，她使许多妇女模仿她对宙斯所做的事。

就是那市场（谁会相信呢？）也是利于丘比特的，随他怎么喧闹，一缕情焰却从那里生出来。在供奉维纳斯的云石的神殿下，阿比阿斯用飞泉来射到空中。在那个地方，有许多法学家为丘比特所缚，而这些能保障别人的却不能保障自己。时常地，在这个地方，就是那最善辩的人也缺乏了辞令，新的利益占据着他，使他不得不为自己的利害而辩论。在邻近，维纳斯在她的殿上以窘态笑着，不久前还是保护别人的，现在却只希望受人保护了。可是尤其应在戏场和它的半圆的座位中撒你的网：这些是最富于好机会的地方。在那里，你可以找到某个勾动你，某个你可以欺骗，某个不过是朵过

---

①即达那俄斯的女儿们，一共有五十个，均嫁给堂兄弟，她除了幼女许珀耳涅斯特拉外，都受父亲的指使，在婚夜中杀了她们的新郎。

②美少年，维纳斯的情人，为野猪所伤而死。为纪念他，每年人们在城中游行，抬吊床，上置阿多尼斯蜡像，覆盖鲜花，女人唱哀歌直到早晨，蜡像投入海中。

③指伊希斯，埃及繁殖女神。在希腊神话中称伊俄，被宙斯所恋，天后赫拉将她变作一头母牛。伊俄在尼罗河边为宙斯生下了儿子厄帕福斯，他后来成为埃及国王。当地人民敬爱伊俄，把她尊为女神。

■ 达那俄斯家的姐妹们 沃特豪斯

　　——达那俄斯的女儿们犯下罪行，在死后永远受到惩罚，永无止境地往无底桶里灌水。

路的闲花，某个你可以和她发生久长的关系。好像蚂蚁在长阵中来来往往地载着它们的食品谷子，或是像那些蜜蜂找到了它们的猎品香草时，轻飞在茴香和花枝上。女子也如此，浓妆艳服着，忙着向那群众走去的戏场去；她们的数目往往使我选择为难。她们是去看的，可是她们尤其是去被看的，这在贞洁是一个危险的地方，这是你开端的啊，罗穆卢斯①，你将烦恼混到游艺中，掳掠萨宾族的女子给你的战士做妻子。

那时垂幕还没有装饰云石的戏场，番红花汁还未染红舞台。从巴拉丁山的树上采下来的树叶的彩带是不精致的剧场的唯一的装饰品。在分段的草地的座位上，人们都坐着，用树叶漫遮着他们的头发。每个人向自己周围观望，注意他所渴望的少女，在心中悄悄地盘旋着万虑千思。

当在号角声中一个狂剧令人用脚在平地上顿了三下时，在人们的欢呼声中，罗穆卢斯便发下暗号给他部下夺取各人的猎品。他们突然发出那泄露阴谋的呼声奔向前去，用他们的贪婪的手伸向年轻的处女身上。正如一群胆小的鸽子奔逃在老鹰之前，正如一只小

---

①罗马的建设者和第一个国王，曾吩咐他的部下在一次大型庆典中抢劫萨宾人的妇女。

■ 萨宾妇女被劫　普桑

绵羊见了狼影儿奔逃，萨宾的女子们也一样地战栗着。当她们看见
那些横蛮的战士向她们扑过来时，她们全都脸色惨白了：因为她们
都很惊慌，虽然惊慌的表现是各不相同的。有的自己抓着自己的头
发，有的坐在位子上晕过去了；这个默默地哭泣，那个徒然地喊着
她的母亲；其余或是呜咽着，或是惊呆了；有的不动地站着，有的

想逃走。人们便牵着那些女子，注定于她们婚床的猎品，有许多因为惊慌而格外显得美丽了。假如有一个女子太反抗，不肯服从那抢她的人，他便抱她起来，热情地将她紧贴在胸口，向她说："为什么用眼泪来损了你的妙目的光辉呢？凡是你父亲用来对你母亲的，我便用来对你。"

哦，罗穆卢斯！只有你能适当地奖赏你的士兵，为了这种奖品，我很愿意投到你的旗帜之下。这是一定的。由于对这古老习俗的忠实，直到现在，剧场还设着为美人们的陷阱。

更不要忘了那骏马竞赛的跑马场。这个聚集着无数群众的竞技场，是有很多机会的。用不着做手势来表示你的秘密，而点头也是不需要的，去表示含有一种特别作用。你去并排坐在她身旁，越贴近越妙，这是不妨的。狭窄的位子使她和你挤得很紧，她没有法子，在你却幸福极了。于是你便找一个起因和她谈话，起初先和她说几句普通的常谈。骏马进了竞技场，你便急忙地去问她马的主人的名字；随便她喜欢哪一匹马，你立刻就要附和她。可是，当那以壮士相斗作先导的赛神会的长行列① 进来时，你便兴高采烈地对她

————————

　　① 赛神会上，人们将神祇的像放在车中或在肩舆上，从宙斯神殿出来，穿过市场和牲口市场，然后到竞技场来，在场中绕一圈。

■ 卡瑞卡拉与盖塔 阿尔玛-达德玛

的保护人维纳斯喝彩。假如，偶然有一点尘埃飞到你的美人的胸口，你便轻轻地用手指拂去它；假如没有尘埃，你也尽管去拂拭：总之，你应当去借用那些冠冕堂皇的由头。她的衣裙是曳在地上吗？你将它揭起来，使得没有东西可以弄脏它。为了你这种殷勤，她会一点不怒地给你一个瞻仰她的腿的恩惠作报偿了。此外，你便当注意坐在她后面的看客，恐怕那伸得太长的膝踝会碰着了她的肩头。这些琐细的事情能笼络住她们轻盈的灵魂：多少多情的男子在一个美女身旁成功，就因为他小心地安好一个坐垫，用一把扇子为她摇风，或者放一张踏脚在她的纤足下。这一切获取新爱情的好机会，你都可以在竞技场和为结怨的烦虑所变作忧愁的市场中找到。丘比特时常欢喜在那儿作战。在那里，那看着别人伤痕的人，自己却感到受了伤；他说话，他为这个或是那个相扑人和别人打赌，他刚接触对方的手，他摆出东道去问谁得胜，忽然一支飞快的箭射透了他；他呼号了一声；于是起初是看斗的看客，如今自己变成牺牲者之一了。

不久之前，恺撒①给我们看那海战的戏，在那里，波斯的战舰和刻克洛普斯的儿郎②的战舰交战，那时两性的青年从各处跑来看这戏；罗马在那时好像是个世界的幽会地。在这人群中，谁没有找到一个恋爱的对象呢？啊！多少的人被一缕异国的情焰烧得焦头烂额！

可是恺撒准备去统一全世界了。现在，东方的远地啊，你们将属于我们了。帕提亚人③啊，你们就要受罚了。克拉苏④，在你的墓中享乐啊；而你们，不幸落在蛮族手中的旗帜啊，你们的复仇者⑤已前进了。

恺撒年纪还很轻的时候，他就有英雄的气概，虽则还是个孩子，他却已指挥那孩子力所不及的军队。怯懦的人们，不要去计算神祇的年龄吧：在恺撒们中，勇敢是超过年岁的。他们的神明的天才是走在时间的前面而发着怒，不耐那迟缓的长大。还是一个小

---

① 指恺撒·屋大维·奥古斯都（公元前63—公元14），是盖乌斯·尤利乌斯（公元前100—前44）的侄子。

② 刻克洛普斯，是雅典的创立者；刻克洛普斯的儿郎指雅典人。

③ 古代民族，罗马的敌人。

④ 罗马大将（约公元前115—前53），前"三头政治"之一，被帕提亚人谋杀。

⑤ 盖乌斯·恺撒，绰号"小兵靴"，奥古斯都的曾孙，当时只有二十岁，做了国王后，变成暴君。他的名言是："让他们恨我，但是让他们怕我。"这是他对臣仆的态度，后为自己的臣仆谋杀。

小的婴孩，梯林斯的英雄① 已经用他的手扼死两条蛇了：他从小就做宙斯的肖子了。而你，老是童颜的巴克斯②，你是多么伟大啊，当战败的印度战栗在你的松球杖③ 前时！

孩子啊，这是在你祖先的保护之下和用你祖先的勇气，你将带起兵来，又将在你祖先的保护之下和用你祖先的勇气战胜他人：一个如此的开端方能与你的鸿名相符。今日的青年王侯，有一朝你将做元老院议长。你有许多弟兄，为那对你弟兄们的侮辱报仇啊。你有一个父亲，拥护你父亲的权力啊。交付你兵权的是国父，也是你自己的父亲；只有仇敌，他才会篡窃父亲的王位④。你呢，佩着神圣的武器，他呢，佩着背誓的箭。人们会看见，在你的旗帜前，神圣的正义走着。本来屈于理的，他们当然屈于兵力了！愿我的英雄将东方的财富带到拉丁姆⑤ 来。

马尔斯神⑥，还有你，恺撒神，在他出发时，助他一臂的神力吧，因为你们两个中一个已经成神了，另一个一朝也将成神的。

---

① 指赫拉克勒斯，梯林斯是他的家乡。
② 酒神，曾被赫拉放逐，漫游各地。
③ 酒神巴克斯的杖，杖端为松球，缠以葡萄蔓及常春藤，故名。
④ 指帕提亚王弗拉特五世，弑父奥洛特基位。
⑤ 罗马所在的地方。
⑥ 战神。宙斯和赫拉的儿子，维纳斯的情人。

是的，我预先测到了，你将战胜的，我许下一个心愿为你制一篇诗，在那里我的嘴很会为你找到流利的音调。我将描写你全身披挂，用一篇理想的演说鼓励起你的士卒。我希望我的诗能配得上你的英武！我将描写那帕提亚人反身而走，罗马人挺胸追逐，追逐敌人时从马上发出箭来。哦，帕提亚人，你想全师而退，可是你战

■ 扼死两条蛇的赫拉克勒斯

败后还剩下些什么呢？帕提亚人啊，从此以后马尔斯只给你不吉的预兆了。

　　世人中之最美者，有一朝我们将看见你满披着黄金①，驾着四匹白马回到我们城下。在你的前面，走着那些颈上系着铁链的敌将们，他们已不能像从前一样地逃走了。青年和少女都将快乐地来参与这个盛会，这一天将大快人心。那时假如有个少女问你那人们背

---

①凯旋者披着的外袍是绛红色又缀着金星。

着的画图上的战败的王侯的名字，什么地方，什么小川，你应当完完全全地回答她，而且要不等她问就说，即使有些是你所不知道的，你也当好像很熟悉地说出来。这就是幼发拉底河，那在额上缠着芦苇的；那披着深蓝色的假发的，就是底格里斯河；那些走过来的，说他们是亚美尼亚人；这女子就是波斯，它的第一个国王是达娜厄①的儿子；这是一座在阿契美尼斯②的子孙的谷中的城。这个囚徒或者那个囚徒都是将士；假如你能够，你便可以一个个地照他们的脸儿取名字，至少要和他们相合的。

　　筵席宴会中也有绝好的机会，人们在那里所找到的不只是饮酒的欢乐。在那里，红颊的丘比特将巴克斯的双臂拥在他纤细的臂间。待到他的翼翅为酒所浸湿时，沉重不能飞的丘比特不动地停留在原处了。可是不久他便摇动他的湿翅，于是那些心上沾着这种炎热的露水的人便不幸了。酒将心安置在温柔中使它易于燃烧；烦虑全消了，被狂饮所消去了。于是欢笑来了；于是穷人也鼓起勇气，自信已是富人了，更没有痛苦、不安，额上的皱纹也平复下去，心花怒放，而那在今日是如此稀罕的爽直又把矫饰驱逐了。在那里，青年人的心是常被

①指居鲁士，波斯开国者。
②达娜厄的祖父，阿契美尼斯的子孙指波斯人。

少女所缚住的；酒后的维纳斯，更是火上加油。可是你切莫轻信那欺人的灯光：为要评断美人，夜和酒都不是好的评判者。

那是在日间，在天光之下，帕里斯看见那三位女神，对维纳斯说："你胜过你的两个敌人，维纳斯。"[1]黑夜抹杀了许多污点，又隐藏了许多缺陷。在那个时候，任何女人都似乎是美丽的了。别人评断宝石和红绫是在日间的，所以评断人体的线条和容貌也需在日间。

■ 罗马洗浴风俗 阿尔玛-达德玛

我可要计算计算那猎美人的一切的汇集处吗？我不如去计算海沙的数目吧。我可要说那巴亚[2]，巴亚的沿岸和那滚着发烟的硫黄泉的浴池吗？在出浴时，许许多多洗浴人的心中都受了伤创，又喊

---

①帕里斯将象征"最美丽者"的金苹果交给维纳斯时所说的话。
②纳泊尔湾中的一座城，有很多温泉，以罗马人在那里筑的许多华丽浴场出名。

着："这受人称颂的水并没有像别人所说的那样合于卫生之道。"

离罗马城不远，便是狄安娜①的神殿，荫着树木，这个主权是赤血和干戈换来的。因为她是处女，因为她怕丘比特的箭，这女神已经伤了她的许多信徒，后来还将伤许多。

在哪里选择你的爱情的目的物？在哪里布你的网？到现在那驾在一个不平衡的车轮的车上的塔利亚②已指示给你了。如今我所要教你的是如何去笼络住那你所爱的人儿，我的功课最要紧的地方就在这里。各地的多情人，望你们当心听我，愿我的允诺找到一个顺利的演说场。

第一，你须得要坚信任何女子都是可以到手的：你将取得她们；只要布你的网就是了。假如女子会不容纳男子的挑逗，春天会没有鸟儿的歌声，夏天会没有蝉声的高唱，野兔子会赶跑梅拿鲁思③的狗。你以为她是不愿的，其实她心中却早已暗暗地愿意了。偷偷摸摸的恋爱在女子看来正是和男子看来一样的有味儿的，但是男子不很知道矫作，女子却将她们的心情掩饰得很好。假如男子们都不先出手，那被屈服的女子立刻就出手了。在那芳草地上，多情地呼着雄牛的是

---

① 月神和狩猎女神。
② 九缪斯之一，司喜剧和牧歌。
③ 阿尔迦第亚的一座山名。

母牛，母马在靠近雄马时又嘶了。在我们人类中，热情是格外节制些，不奔放些；人类的情焰是不会和自然之理相背的，我可要说皮布丽斯①吗？她为了她的哥哥，烧起了那罪恶的情焰，然后自缢了，勇敢地去责罚自己的罪恶。密拉②爱她的父亲，可是并非用一种女儿对父亲的爱情，如今她已将她的羞耻隐藏在那裹住她的树皮中了。她成了芳树，倾出眼泪来给我们做香料，又保留住这不幸女子的名字。

在遮满了树丛的伊达③的幽谷中，有一头白色的雄牛，这是群牛中的光荣。它的额上有一点小黑斑，只有这一点，在两角之间，身上其余完全是乳白色的。克诺索斯④和启道奈阿⑤的母牛都争以得到被它压在背上为荣幸。

帕西法厄⑥渴望做它的情妇，她嫉恨着那些美丽的母牛。这是个已经证实的事实；那坐拥百城的克里特⑦，专事欺人说谎的克里

---

① 水仙，爱上她的哥哥，追逐他到了很多地方，由于得不到爱情自缢而死，化作一孔泉水。
② 她父亲是客涅阿斯，维纳斯为了报复，叫她爱上了自己的父亲。奥维德《变形记》中有记载。
③ 克里特山名。
④ 克里特名城。
⑤ 克里特北部名城。
⑥ 弥诺斯的妻子。
⑦ 一小岛名。

■ 阿多尼斯的诞生（局部）提香
　　——画面一侧是密拉和她的父亲，暗示了乱伦主题；另一侧是一群人把婴儿阿多尼斯从树干中解救出来的情景，那棵没药树是他的母亲密拉变成的。

特，也不能否认这事实。别人说那帕西法厄用不惯熟的手，亲自摘鲜叶和嫩草给那雄牛吃，而且，为要伴着它，她连自己的丈夫都不想起了：一头雄牛竟胜于弥诺斯。帕西法厄，你为什么穿着这样豪华的衣裳？你的情夫是不懂得你的富丽的。当你到山上去会牛群时，为什么拿着一面镜子？你为什么不停地理你的发丝？多么愚笨！至少相信你的镜子吧：它告诉你，你不是一头母牛。你是多么希望在你的额上长出两只角来啊！假如你是爱弥诺斯的，不要去找情人吧，或者，假如你要欺你的丈夫，至少也得和一个"人"通奸啊。可是偏不如此。那王后遗弃了龙床，奔波于树林之间，像一个被阿沃尼阿的神祇[1] 所激动的跳神诸女[2] 一样。多少次，她把那妒嫉

_____

　　[1] 指巴克斯，酒神的母亲塞墨勒住在鲍艾沃帝阿的都城忒拜，鲍艾沃帝阿古名阿沃尼阿。
　　[2] 指巴克斯节的巫女。她们披散头发，戴常春藤编成的帽子，手中拿着松球杖，边跳舞，边狂喊，边奔跑。

的目光投在一头母牛身上，说着："为什么会得我心上的人儿的欢心？你看它在它前面的草地上多么欢跃着啊！这蠢货无疑地自以为这样可以觉得更可爱了。"她说着便立刻吩咐将那头母牛从牛群中牵出来，或者使它低头在轭下，或是使它倒毙在一个没有诚心的献祀的祭坛下。于是她充满了欢乐，将她的情敌的心脏拿在手中。她屡次杀戮了她的情敌，假说是去息神祇之怒，又拿着它们的心脏说着："现在你去娱我的情郎吧！"

有时她愿意做欧罗巴①，有时她羡慕着伊俄的命运：因为一个是母牛，还有一个是因为被一头雄牛负在背上的。可是为一头木母牛的像所蛊惑，那牛群的王使帕西法厄怀了孕，而她所产出来的果子泄露出她的羞耻的主动。

假如那另一个克里特女子会不去爱梯厄斯忒斯②（在妇人专爱着一个男子是一桩多难的事啊！），人们不会看见福玻斯在他的中路停止了，回转他的车子，将他的马驾向东方。尼索斯的女儿③，因为

---

① 宙斯爱上了欧罗巴，变成一头可爱的白牛，引诱欧罗巴戏跨在它身上，宙斯便背着她到克里特去，在那里他们生了三个孩子。

② 迈锡尼王阿特柔斯之弟。他勾引嫂子阿厄罗佩（前文提到的"克里特女子"），并企图篡夺王位，事败后二人出逃。

③ 指斯库拉，是尼索斯的女儿。她割去她父亲头上系着命运和生命的头发给她的爱人弥诺斯，而弥诺斯是她父亲的敌人。她后来被变作一个腰上长着恶狗的怪物。

■ 代达罗斯为帕西法厄造木牛　庞贝壁画

割了她父亲的光辉的头发，变成了一个腰上长着许多恶狗的怪物。阿特柔斯的儿子①，在地上脱逃了马尔斯，在海上脱逃了涅普顿②，终究做了他的妻子的不幸的牺牲者。谁不曾将眼泪洒在那烧着爱费拉③的克瑞乌莎④的情焰上，和在那染着血的杀了自己的孩子的母亲⑤身上？阿明托尔的儿子菲尼克斯⑥悲哭他的眼

　　①指阿伽门农，特洛伊战争中希腊军队的主将，回国后被他不忠的妻子克吕泰墨斯特拉伙同情夫埃癸斯托斯谋杀。
　　②海神，相当于希腊神话中的波塞冬。
　　③科林斯古名，希腊的一座城。
　　④科林斯的公主，伊阿宋的妻子。
　　⑤指美狄亚，伊阿宋的前妻，魔女。曾帮助伊阿宋取金羊毛，后来伊阿宋爱上了克瑞翁的女儿克瑞乌莎，她很愤怒，送了施过魔法的嫁衣和花冠，这两件东西烧死了克瑞乌莎。同时，美狄亚把自己和伊阿宋所生的孩子也杀死了。
　　⑥阿明托尔的儿子，阿明托尔的妾诬陷他，被阿明托尔听信，挖去了他的双眼。

睛的失去。希波吕托斯①的骏马，在你们的惊恐中，将你们主人的躯体弄碎了！菲纽斯②，你为什么挖去你的无辜的孩子们的眼睛啊？那报应将重复落在你头上了。

情人中无羁的热情的放荡是如此：比我们的还热烈，还奔放。勇敢些，带着必胜之心去上阵。在一千个女子中，能抵拒你的连一个都找不到。随她们容纳也好，拒绝也好，她们总喜欢别人去献好的。即使假定你被拒绝了，这种失败在你是没有危险的。可是你怎会被拒绝呢？一个人常会在新的陶醉中找到欢乐的：别人的东西总比自己的好。别家田中的收获总觉得格外丰饶，邻人的畜群总是格外肥壮的。

你第一个要先和你所逢迎的女子的侍女去结识：那给你进门的方便的就是她。去探听确实，她的女主人是否完全信任她，她是否是女主人的秘密欢乐的忠心同谋者。为要买她到手，许愿和央求一件也少不得；这样你所要求的，她都会给你办到了。一切都

---

① 雅典王忒修斯的儿子。忒修斯和菲德拉结婚后，菲德拉爱上了他前妻的儿子希波吕托斯，但遭到拒绝。菲德拉便失望怨恨地自缢了，留下一卷对于希波吕托斯的诬词。忒修斯看了十分气愤，要求海神波塞冬为他报仇；一天，希波吕托斯驾车到海边去，海上突现一头海怪，他的马大惊，将车子掀翻，希波吕托斯被淹死。

② 忒拜王，听信后妻的谗言，害死了他的儿子们，宙斯降罚于他，使他瞎了眼，而且每次有食物时，都被哈尔庇厄（掠夺者）抢去。

■ 愤怒的美狄亚 德拉克洛瓦
——画中描绘了愤怒的母亲美狄亚杀子的情景。

出于她的高兴。她会选择一个顺利的时候（医生也注意时候的）；要趁她女主人容易说话的时候，最受勾引的时候。在那时，一切都向她微笑着，欢乐在她的眼中发着光，正如金穗在丰田中一样。当心怀欢快时，当它不为忧苦所缚时，它便自然地开放了；那时维纳斯便轻轻地溜了进去。伊利昂[①]一日在愁困之中，它的兵力就和希腊的兵力对抗，那迎入藏着战士的木马进城的那天[②]，却是一个快乐的日子啊。你更要选她受对头侮辱而啜泣的时候，使她可以要你做她的报复者。早晨，正在理发时，侍女触怒了她。为了你，她借此张帆打桨，低声说，

————

① 指特洛伊。
② 指希腊人以木马计攻入特洛伊城。

还叹息着："我不相信你会恩怨分明的。"于是她便说起了你，她为你说了一篇动心的话，她说你将为情而死。可是你应当迅速从事，恐怕风就要停、帆就要落。怒气正如薄冰一样，一期待就消化了。

你要问我了：先得到侍女的欢心可有用吗？这种办法是很偶然的。有的侍女用这办法果然使她格外热心为你出力，有的却反不热心了。这个为你照料她女主人的恩情，那个却将你留住自己受用了。大胆者得成功：即使这句话会助你的勇气，照我的意见，免之为善。因为我是不向悬崖绝壁去找我的路的。请我来做引导的人，是不会走入迷途的。可是当侍女传书递简时，她的美丽媚你不下于她的热忱，你总须以得到那女主人为先；侍女自然随后就来了；可是你的爱却不应该从她开始。

只有一个劝告，假如你对于我所教的功课有几分信心，假如我的话不被狂风吹到大海去，千万不要冒险，否则也得弄个彻底。一朝这件风流案中侍女有了一半份儿，她便不会叛你了。翼上沾着黐的鸟不能远飞；野猪徒然地在笼住它的网中挣扎；鱼一上了钩，就不能逃脱。那已被你挑逗了的，你须要快快地紧逼，一直到胜利后才放手。可是你要瞒得好好的！假如你对侍女将你的聪敏藏得很好，你的情人所做的一切在你都不成为神秘了。

■ 特洛伊人拖着木马进城

　　相信只有农夫和水手才应当顾虑时机的人，实在是一个大错误。正如不应该一年到头地在那一块会欺骗我们的地上播种，或是不时地将一只小舟放到碧海上去一样，一天到晚地向一个美人进攻也是一样靠不住的。等着一个好机会，人们是时常很好地达到目的。假如你在她的生日或是那历书上维纳斯欢喜紧搂她的爱人马尔斯的日子^①，当竞技场已不像从前一样地装饰着些小雕像，却陈设着败王的战利品

————————

　　①指维纳斯节，4月1日，紧接三月。三月是战神的节日。

时，你就得停止进行了。于是凄戚的冬天来了，于是百莱阿代斯①近了，于是温柔的山羊沉到大洋中去了②。那便是休息的好时候，谁要不自量力到海上去，谁就要碎了他的船，甚至性命都难保。着手于那使人流那样多的眼泪的，阿里阿河③染红了拉丁族的血的日子，或是在巴莱斯底那的叙利亚人每周所庆祝的安息日。你要十分当心你的腻友的生日，你更要把那些要送礼的日子视作禁

■ 维纳斯和战神马尔斯的雕像

忌日。你想脱兔是徒然的，她总会弄到些你的礼物的；女人总是精于种种搜刮她的热情的情人的钱的艺术。一个穿着长袍的贩子会到你情人的家里去，她老是预备着购买的，他将在坐着的你的面前，摊开他的货品来。于是她，为了给你一个显出你的鉴赏力的机会，要求你为

---

① 指七星落时，即11月8日至11日。
② 指10月初。
③ 拉丁姆的一条河，公元前389年，罗马人在那里被高卢人打败。

她看一看，随后她会给你几个甜吻，随后她恳求你买几件。她会发誓说这些已够她几年之用了，而今天她正用得到，今天是一个机会。你说你身边没有带钱是无用的：她会请你开一张票子，那时你会懊悔你知书识字了。当她为要你的礼物，好像做生日地预备起点心来时——而且这生日又是每次当她需要什么东西时做的——怎样办呢？当她假说失了一件东西，含愁而来，泣诉她丢失了一块耳上的宝石时，怎样办呢？情人们老是向你要许多东西，这些东西她们说不久就会还你的；可是一朝到了她们手中，你再也莫想她们还你了。在你是受了这么大的损失，别人却一点也不感激你。

先在几个精磨的板上写个温柔的简帖儿去探路。要使这第一个函札使她知道你的心情。上面要写着殷勤的颂词和动情的话，而且不要管你的身份，你加上那最低微的恳求。赫克托耳的尸体之所以能还给普里阿摩斯①，也就为那老人的恳求动了阿喀琉斯的心。神祇之怒都为柔顺的声音所动。

答应啊，答应啊；这是不值得什么的；任何人都是富于允许的。那希望，当人们加上信心时，是能经久的：这是个欺人的女神，但是却很有用。假如你送了些礼物给你的情人，你就会找不到便宜

---

① 特洛伊王，赫克托耳之父。

了：就是欺骗了你，她也不会有所损失的。你总得常带着正要送她东西的样子，可是永不要送她。不茁的田就是如此地常欺骗了它的主人的希望；赌徒也就是如此地在不再输的希望中不停地输出，而偶然的运气又诱惑着他的贪婪的手。那最难的一点，那细巧的工作，就是不赠礼物而得到美人的眷顾，于是，她为了要不虚掷她所赠与的东西的价值，她便不能拒绝了。将这满篇柔情的简帖儿发出去，去探她的心，去开一条路。几个写在苹果上的字欺骗了绮第佩①，于是这不知内幕的少女在朗读它时，为她自己的言语所缚住了。

研究美文啊，青年罗马人，我这样忠告你们，不仅是为要保护那战战兢兢的被告人：正如人民、严厉的审判官和从人民中选出来的元老院议员，女人也是屈服于辩才的。可是你要将你的诱惑的方法隐藏得很好，不要一下子就显露出你的饶舌来。一切迂腐浅陋的语句都不要用。除了蠢人以外，谁会用一种演说者的口气写信给他的情人呢？一封夸张的信时常造成一种厌恶的主因。你的文体须要自然，你的词句须要简单，可是要婉转，使别人读你这信时，好像听到你的声音一样。

——————————

① 雅典女子。阿工谛乌斯往她脚下扔了一个苹果，上面写着："我凭阿耳忒弥斯宣誓，我将嫁给阿工谛乌斯。"绮第佩高声宣读，被女神听到，不得不嫁给阿工谛乌斯。

假如她拒绝你的简帖儿，将它看也不看一下地送还你，你尽希望她将读它，你要坚持到底。不驯的小牛终究惯于驾犁，倔强的马日久终受制于辔头。在不停地摩擦后，一个铁指环尚会磨损，继续地划着地，那弯曲的犁头终究蚀损。还有什么比石再坚，比水更柔的吗？可是柔水却滴穿了坚石。即使是珀涅罗珀①，只要你坚持到底，日久她总会屈服于你。拜尔迦摩斯②守了很长时间，可是终究被夺得了。

　　譬如她读了你的信而不愿回答你，那是她的自由。你只要使她继续读你的情书就是了。她既然很愿意读，她不久就会愿意回答了。一切都是按部就班地来的。你或许先会接到一封不顺利的复信，在信上她请你停止追求。正当她求你莫惹她时，她却恐惧着你依她照办，而希望你坚持到底。追求啊，不久你就会如愿以偿了。

　　假如当你遇到你的情人躺在她的床中的时候，你便走过去，好像是偶然似的；而且，为了怕你的话语被一个不谨慎的人听了去，你便尽你所能地用模棱两可的手势来达意。假如她在一个广大的穹

---

　　①奥德修斯的妻子，以贞洁出名，在奥德修斯漂流的十年中，一直等待着奥德修斯的归来。
　　②特洛伊要塞。

门下闲步，你亦应当挨上去和她一起闲游。有时走在她前面，有时走在她后面；有时加紧了脚步，有时放慢了脚步。你不要为了从人群中走出，从这柱石赶到那柱石去紧贴她而害羞。不要让她独自仪态万方地坐在戏场中：在那里，她的袒露的玉臂将给你一个动情的奇观。在那里，你可以凝视着她，安闲地欣赏她，你可以向她打手势，做媚

■ 丘比特和赛姬 安东尼奥·卡诺瓦

眼。对那扮少女的曲伶人① 喝彩；对那扮演情人的更要喝彩。她站起来，你便站起来；她一直坐着，你也坐着不要动；你须懂得依着你的情人的兴致去花费你的时间。

可是不要用热铁去烫你的头发，或是用浮石去砾你的皮肤。这些事让那些用弗里吉亚人的仪式哼着歌词颂西布莉虞斯山的女神的教士们② 去做吧。一种不加修饰的美是合宜于男子的：当弥诺斯的

---

① 指扮演少女的男子。
② 西布莉虞斯，是弗里吉亚的一座山，山的女神是西布莉，是弗里吉亚人的女神，后为罗马人所崇奉；她的教士全都被阉割过。

女儿①被忒修斯掠去的时候，忒修斯并没有将自己的头发用针簪在鬓边。希波吕托斯虽然外表不事修饰，却被菲德拉所爱。那森林的荒野寄客阿多尼斯终究得到一个女神的心②。你须要爱清洁，不要怕在马尔斯场锻炼身体而晒黑了你的皮肤。把你的宽袍弄得好好的，不要沾污。舌上不要留一点舌苔，齿上不要留一点齿垢。你的脚不要套着太大的鞋子；不要使你的剪得不好的头发矗起在你头上。却要请一副老练的手来整理你的头发和胡子；你的指甲须剪得很好而且干净，在鼻孔中不要使鼻毛露出；不要使那难受的气息从一张臭嘴里吐出来，当心那公羊臊气使人难闻。其余的修饰，你让与那些年轻的媚娘或是那些反自然地求得男子眷恋的男子去做吧。

可是这里利倍尔③呼召他的诗人了，他也是保护有情人又加惠于那些他自己也燃烧着的爱情的。

纳克索斯的孩子④发狂地在荒滩上彷徨着，在第阿⑤小岛被海波冲击的地方。她刚从睡眠中脱身出来，只穿了一条薄薄的下衣，她的

---

① 指阿里阿德涅，是弥诺斯和帕西法厄的女儿，用丝线帮助忒修斯杀死弥诺陶洛斯逃出迷宫，后被忒修斯抛弃。
② 女神指维纳斯。
③ 古意大利神祇，相当于罗马神话中的巴克斯。
④ 指阿里阿德涅，她住在纳克索斯。
⑤ 纳克索斯对面的一个小岛。

■ 阿里阿德涅　沃特豪斯
　　——阿里阿德涅还在熟睡，忒修斯已经领着众人离开了纳克索斯岛。

脚跣露着，她的棕色头发乱飘在肩头，她向着那听不到她的声音的海
波哭诉忒修斯的残忍，而眼泪是满溢在那可怜的少女的娇颜上。

　　她且哭且喊，可是哭和喊在她都是很配的，她的眼泪使她格外
娇艳可人了。那个不幸的人儿拍着胸说："那负心人弃我而去了，
我怎么办呢？"她说："我怎么办呢？"忽然铙钹声在整个海岸上
高响起来了，狂热的手打着鼓声也起来了。她吓倒了，而她的声音
也停止了，她已失去知觉了。这里，那些披头散发的跳舞诸女来

了；轻捷的萨提洛斯①们，神的先驱来了，这里，酩酊的老人西勒诺斯②来了，他挂在那弯曲在重负之下的驴子的鬃毛上，几乎要跌下来了。当他追着那一边逃避他一边向他啰唆的跳神诸女的时候，当这个拙骑士用木棒打着那只长耳兽的时候，忽然滑了下来，跌了个倒栽葱。那些萨提洛斯喊着："嘿，起来啊，老伯伯，起来啊！"那时那神祇③高坐在缠着葡萄蔓的车上，用金勒驾驭着那驯虎。

那少女把颜色、忒修斯的记忆和声音同时都失去了。她想逃了三次，可是恐惧心缠了她三次脚。她战栗着，正如被风飘动的稻草和在沼泽中的芦苇一样。可是那神祇却向她说："我是来向你供献忠诚的爱情的，不要怕吧，克诺索斯的女孩子，你将做巴克斯的妻子了，我拿天来给你做礼物。在天上，你将成一颗人们所瞻望的星，你的灿烂的冠冕将在那里做没有把握的舵工的指导。"他这样说着，又恐怕那些老虎吓坏了阿里阿德涅，便从车上跳下来（他的足迹印在地上）；把那失魂的公主紧抱在胸怀，他将她举了起来。她怎样会抵抗呢？一个神祇的权能难道还有什么为难的事吗？有的

---

① 巴克斯的伴侣。
② 巴克斯的保护人和随从，秃顶，骑驴，总是醉着。
③ 指酒神巴克斯。

唱着催妆曲，有的喊着："曷许斯，曷荷艾。"① 那年轻的新妇和神祇是如此地在神圣的榻上相合的。

因此你便当置身于有巴克斯的礼物的华筵中，假如一个女子是坐在你旁边，和你同坐在一张榻上，你便祷告那在夜间供奉的夜的神祇②，求他不要把你弄醉。于是你便可以用隐约的言语向她说出温柔的情话，她将毫不困难地猜度出你的意思来，用一点酒漫意地画着多情的表记，使她在桌子上看出她是你的心上的情人来，你的凝视着她的眼睛，须要向她露出你的情焰来。用不着语言，脸儿自有其雄辩的声音和语言。她的嘴唇啜过的酒杯你须得第一个抢来，而在她喝过的那一边上，你也喝着。她的手指所触过的一切的菜肴，你去拿来，而在拿的时候，摸一摸她的手。

喝酒的时候所守的准则是什么呢？我们就要指教你了。你的智慧和你的脚须要时常保持着平衡。尤其是要避免那些因酒而发生的争端，不要轻易和人家斗。不要学那愚蠢地因饮酒过度而致死的欧律提翁③：酒席和酒只应当引起一种温柔的欢快。假如你嗓子好，你

---

① "曷许斯"是巴克斯的别名；"曷荷艾"是跳神诸女的欢呼声，从别名演变而来。

② 指巴克斯。

③ 半人半马的怪物，因在别人的婚礼上想对新娘无礼，而被斗死。

■ 酒神巴克斯和阿里阿德涅　提香

便唱，假如你身段灵活，你便跳舞。一切使人欢乐的，你都要一件件地去做。真醉会惹起旁人的讨厌，假醉在你却十分有用。你的狡猾的舌头要咯咯地吐着不清楚的声音，这样你所做的和你所说的如果有些大胆的地方，人们就可以原谅你。

当酒阑客散的时候，那些客人就给你接近你的美人的方法和机会。你夹在人群中，轻轻地靠近她，用你的手指捏她的身子，用你的脚去碰她的脚。这便是交谈的时光。乡下气的羞态，走远些！机会和维纳斯帮助大胆的人。像你那样会说话当然用不着来请教我们。只要想着开端，辩才便不待思索自然而然地来了。你应当扮着那个情郎的角色，而且在你的言语中，你须要做出受过爱情的伤的样子来，要用尽种种的方法使她坚信，要得到别人的相信并不是很难的：任何女人都自以为配得上被爱的，就是那最丑的女子也卖弄着风姿。况且多少次那起初装作在恋爱的终究真正地恋爱起来了，从矫作而至于实现！年轻的美人们啊，请你们对那些做着爱情的外表给你们看的人们宽大些。这种爱情，起初是扮演的，以后却要变作诚恳的了。你更可以用那些巧妙的阿谀偷偷地得到她的欢心，正如那水流不知不觉地蔽盖了那统治它的河岸一样。你要一点不迟疑地去赞美她的姿容、她的头发、她的团团的指和纤纤的脚。那最贞淑的女子听了那对于她的美的谀辞也要动心，容颜的美就是贞女也要注意的。赫拉和帕拉斯在弗里吉亚树林中不是就为了这个缘故到如今还有意见①吗？你且看这只赫拉的鸟②，假如你赞美它的翎羽，它便开屏了；假如你默默地看着它，它便把它的宝物隐藏着了。在赛车的时候，骏马是喜欢别人对它梳得很好的鬣毛和优美的项颈喝彩的。

　　你须要大胆地发誓，因为引动女人的是誓言，牵了一切的神祇来为你的诚恳作证。宙斯在天上笑着情人们的假誓，又将这些假誓像玩具一样地叫埃俄罗斯③的臣仆带去撤销了。宙斯也常对着

---

　　①指帕里斯裁判维纳斯为最美丽者之事。帕拉斯即希腊神话中的智慧女神雅典娜。
　　②指一只孔雀。
　　③风神。

■ 帕里斯的裁判 鲁本斯

斯提克斯^①向赫拉立假誓的：他在今日当然加惠于那些学他的样的人们的。诸神祇的存在是有用的，而且，因为有用，我们且相信他们是存在的吧。在他们的祭坛前，我们应该浪费我们的香和

———————————

①冥土中的一条河，诸神常对着它发誓。

酒。他们不是沉浸在一个无知觉的、和睡眠相似的休息中的。你要过着一种纯洁的生活，神祇是看着你的。还了那寄存在你那儿的寄托物，依着那信心所吩咐你的条例，切莫作恶，使你的手清洁而不染着人类的血。假如你是聪明人，你要玩也只玩着女人。你这样做可以无罪的，只要你是出于诚意。欺骗那欺骗你的人们。大部分的女子都是不忠实的，她们安排着陷阱，让她们自己坠下去吧。

有人说埃及曾经一连大旱过九年，一滴润田的水都没有。于是德拉西乌斯①前来找布西里斯②，对他说他能够平息宙斯的怒，只要在宙斯的祭坛上浇上一个异乡人的血就好了。布西里斯回答他说："很好，你将做那供献给宙斯的第一个牺牲，你将做那把雨水给埃及的异乡人。"法拉里斯③也使人在铜牛中烧死残忍的培里鲁斯④，那个不幸的发明者用自己的血浇着他亲手所做的成绩。公正的双料的例子！其实将那罪恶的制造者用他们自己所造的东西来处死是再公正也没有了，以伪誓答伪誓是公平的法则，那欺诈的女人，应当像她所做过的一般受人的欺诈！

---

① 一个神明的启泊鲁斯岛人。
② 古埃及国王，异常残忍。
③ 公元6世纪阿格里于顿国暴君。
④ 雅典金匠，为法拉里斯铸铜牛，以烧死犯罪的人，他被暴君第一个烧死。

眼泪也是有用的，它会软化金刚石。你须要使你的情人看见你泪珠儿断颊横腮。可是假如你流不出眼泪来的时候（因为眼泪不是随叫随到的），你便用你的手将你的眼眶儿弄湿了。

哪一个有经验的男子不把接吻混到情语中去呢？你的美人拒绝，随她拒绝，你做你的就是了。起初她或许会抵拒，会叫你"坏坏子"；可是就正当她在抵拒的时候，她实在心愿屈服。可是你须得不要用拙笨的接吻碰痛了她的娇嫩的唇儿，给她一个口实说你粗蛮。你得到一个亲吻而不去取得其余的，你便坐失了那她允许你的恩惠了。

在一度接吻之后，你还等着什么来实现你的一切心愿呢。多么可怜啊！牵制住你的不是羞耻，却是一种愚昧笨拙。你会说，这不是对她施行强暴了吗？可是这种强暴正是情人所欢喜的，她们欢喜给人的东西，她们也愿人们去夺取。被爱情的盗窃所突然地以力取得的情人反而享乐着这种盗窃，这种横蛮在她们是像送她们礼物一样的称心。当她从一个别人可以袭得她的挣扎中无瑕地脱身出来的时候，她很可以在脸上装作快活，其实却是满肚子不高兴。福柏①

---

① 福柏的妹妹是希拉伊拉，她们的父亲吕西普斯将她们许给伊达斯和林开斯兄弟。海伦的兄弟卡斯托耳、波吕丢刻斯迷恋她们，将她们抢去。事见奥维德的《年代纪》。

■ 劫夺吕西普斯的女儿们　鲁本斯

曾经受过强暴，她的妹妹也做了强暴的牺牲；可是她们两个却爱那对她们施强暴的人。

一个大家知道的故事，可是却很值得一讲，那就是斯库洛斯的少女①和海蒙尼亚的英雄②的结合。在伊达山上，那个女神③已经对她的敌人唱凯旋歌，已经报偿了称她最美的人了；一个新媳妇已经从远地里来到普里阿摩斯的家中了，而在伊利昂的城垣中已关进了一个希腊的妻子了。全希腊的王侯都发誓为受辱的丈夫④报仇，因为一个人的侮辱已变为大家的侮辱了。那时阿喀琉斯（假如他听了他母亲的请求，那是多么的羞耻啊！）把自己的男性隐藏在女人穿的长衫子里。你做什么啊，埃阿科斯的孙子？纺羊毛不是你的本分。你应当从雅典娜⑤的别一种艺术中找出你的光荣来。这些女红篮子你管它干吗？你的手是注定拿盾的。为什么你拿梭子，难道要用这个扑倒赫克托耳吗？把这个纺锤丢得远一些，你的手是应该举

①指斯库洛斯岛吕科墨得斯王的女儿得伊达弥亚。
②指阿喀琉斯，为躲避战争被母亲藏在吕科墨得斯的王宫中，期间与得伊达弥亚发生关系。
③指维纳斯。
④指海伦之夫墨涅拉俄斯。
⑤她不仅是智慧女神，还是战争女神。

起贝利翁山的矛^①来的。

　　有朝一日，在同一张床上睡着一个王族的女儿^②，她发现了她的伴侣是一个男子，于是她受到强暴了。她是屈服于武力的（至少应当作如是想），可是她并不因为屈服于武力而发怒。当阿喀琉斯已经匆匆要出发的时候，她常常对他说"不要走"，因为那时阿喀琉斯已经放下了梭子去取兵器了。那个所谓"强暴"那时到哪里去了？得伊达弥亚，你为什么用一种抚爱的语气来留你的羞辱的主动者呢？

　　是的，羞耻心禁止女人先来爱抚男子，但是当男子开始先去爱抚她时，她是非常喜欢的。自然啦，少年人对于自己的体格的美有一种太自负的信心了，他等着女子先上手。应当是男子开始的，应当是男子来说一切的祷词的；他的爱情的祈祷便会被她很好地接受了。你要得到她吗？请求吧。她只希望着这种请求。向她解释你的爱情的原因和来历。宙斯都恳求着走向传说中的女英雄们去，随他如何伟大，没有一个女子会先来挑拨他的。可是你的恳求撞在一种轻蔑别人的骄傲的厌恶上呢，你便不要再固执了，退转身来。多

---

　　①指阿喀琉斯的长矛，其父珀琉斯受赠于启洪，后来传给他。
　　②指得伊达弥亚，阿喀琉斯躲在吕科墨得斯宫中时，扮成女子，很方便地强暴了得伊达弥亚。

少的女子希望着那些溜脱她们
的人而厌恶那些专心侍奉着她
们的人！不要太性急，那你便
不会受人厌恶了。在你的请求
中不要常常泄露出达到最后目
的的希望来，为要使你的爱情
渗透到她的心里，你须得戴着
友谊的假面具。我看见许多不
驯的美人都受了这种驭制法的
骗：她们的朋友不久就变成了
她们的情人。

■ 丘比特和普塞克　弗朗索瓦·热拉尔

　　一张雪白的脸儿是和水
手不配的，海水和日光准会早
把他的脸儿弄成褐色了；它和农夫也是不配的，因为农夫老是在露
天之下，用犁头或是重耙垦着泥土；而你也是一样的，你这在游戏
中谋得橄榄冠的人，生着雪白的皮肤是你的羞耻。可是一切的多情
人都应该是惨白的，因为惨白是爱情的病征，那才是和他相称的

颜色。许多人以为这个并不是没有用的。俄里翁①是惨白的，当他为西黛②所爱在树林里彷徨着的时候，惨白的达佛涅斯③为一个无情的水仙所爱。你更要用你的消瘦显露出你的心的苦痛来，还要不怕羞地用病人的包头布将你的光耀的头发裹住。那由一种剧烈的爱发出的不眠、烦虑、苦痛使一个青年人消瘦。为要达到你的心愿，你要使别人可怜你，要使人一看到你就脱口而出地说："你正在恋爱。"

如今我应该缄默呢，还是应该含愁地看着德行和罪恶相混呢？友谊、善意都只是空虚的字眼。啊啊！你不能毫无危险地向你的友人夸耀你所爱着的人儿；假如他相信了你的颂词，他立刻会变成你的对手了。有人会要对我说："可是那阿克托尔的孙子④并没有玷污了阿喀琉斯的床呀；菲德拉虽然不忠实，庇里托俄斯⑤却没有什么举动呀；皮拉德斯⑥爱着赫耳弥俄涅⑦，他的爱情是和福玻斯之对

---

① 海神之子，英俊的猎人。
② 俄里翁之妻，被赫拉投入地狱。
③ 西西里牧人，牧歌的创造者，与水仙相爱，后因背誓，双目失明，从岩石上坠下而死。
④ 指帕特洛克罗斯，阿喀琉斯的挚友，在特洛伊战争中被赫克托耳杀死。
⑤ 菲德拉的丈夫忒修斯的好友。
⑥ 俄瑞斯忒斯的好友。
⑦ 海伦之女，俄瑞斯忒斯之妻。

于帕拉斯，或是卡斯托耳和波吕丢刻斯之对于廷达瑞俄斯[①] 的女儿
的爱情一样的纯洁。"在今天相信这种奇谈，不啻是希望西河柳结
果子或是到江心去找蜜一样。罪犯是有多少的香饵啊！各人都谋私
自的欢乐，尝着别人的欢乐是格外来得有味儿的。多么可耻啊！一
个有情人所要顾忌的倒不是他的仇敌。你要高枕无忧，你便该避开

———————————

　　① 斯巴达王，海伦之父。

那些你以为对你忠实的朋友。亲戚、兄弟、挚友全不可信托，这些是能给你以极大的恐惧的人。

我就要结束了，可是我要说，女子的脾气都不全是一样的，对于这些不同的性格，你要用千种的方法去引诱。同一块土地不能生出一切的产品：有的宜于葡萄，有的宜于橄榄，有的是种起麦来才有好收成。人心不同，各如其面。伶俐的男子能屈就那各种不同的，像有时变作清波，有时变成狮子，有时变作坚毛的野猪的普罗透斯①一样的脾气。有的鱼是用渔叉叉的，有的鱼是用钩子钩的，有的鱼是用网网的。老是一个方法是不会成功的，应当依照你的情人的年龄而变通。一头老雌鹿能很远地发现别人为它设下的陷阱。假如你在一个初出道儿的女子前显露出太精专，或是在一个忸怩的女子前显露出太冒险，她就立刻不信任你，而小心防范着你了。所以，怕委身于一个规矩男人的女人，总是可耻地坠入一个浪子的怀抱中。

我的一部分的工程已做完，只剩下另一部分要做了。现在我们且抛下了锚停下我们的船吧。

---

① 一个海神，会变幻各种形象。

第二卷

如何保持爱情

On Making Love Last

唱"伊奥·拜盎"①呀，再唱一遍"伊奥·拜盎"呀。我所追求的猎品已投入我的网罗中了。欢乐的有情人，把一个绿色的月桂冠加在我头上，又将我举到阿斯克拉的老人②和梅奥尼亚的盲人③之上吧。正如那脱逃了尚武的阿米克莱城④，一帆风顺地将东道主的妻子⑤带走了的普里阿摩斯的儿子⑥一样；又正如，希波达弥亚⑦啊，那把你载在胜利的车上，将你带到异国去的珀罗普斯一样。青年人，你为什么如此的性急啊？你的船还在大海的中央，离我所引你去的港口还很远啊。我的诗还不够做到把你所爱的人儿放在你的怀间的程度，我的艺术使你取得她，我的艺术也应当使你保持她。得到胜利和保持胜利是同样的要有才能的，其一还有点机会，其一却完全是靠我的艺术的。

现在，塞西拉的女神⑧和你的儿子，请你们帮我啊。现在，你，埃

---

①阿波罗的颂歌。

②指古希腊大诗人赫西奥德。

③指荷马，梅奥尼亚是他的故乡。

④斯巴达东南的一座城。

⑤海伦。

⑥帕里斯。

⑦俄诺马诺斯的女儿。预言说，只有赛车胜过她父亲的人才能娶她为妻。后来珀罗普斯爱上了她，和她的父亲赛车，她贿赂父亲的车夫，弄去了父亲车轮上的辐，使珀罗普斯赢得胜利，也赢得了希波达弥亚。

⑧指维纳斯，塞西拉岛是供奉维纳斯的地方。

■ 诗人的灵感　普桑

拉托①也请你帮我啊，因为你的名字是从爱情来的。我计划着一个大事业，我将说用哪一种艺术人们可以固定丘比特，那个不停地在宇宙中飞翔着的轻躁的孩子。他是轻飘的，他有一双能使他脱逃的翼翅，要

————————

　　① 九缪斯之一，司爱情诗。

使他不飞是很困难的。

　　弥诺斯为了防止他的宾客逃走，在一切的路上都设了防，可是这客人却敢用翼翅来开辟一条新路。当代达罗斯把那个犯罪的母亲的爱情的果子半人半牛的怪物关起来以后，便对弥诺斯说："弥诺斯啊，你是凡人中最公正的，请你赐我回去吧，使我的骨灰葬在我的故土中吧！做了不公正的命运的牺牲者，我不能生活在我的乡土中，至少准许我死在那儿。假如那老人不能得到你的恩准，那么请准许我的儿子回去吧；假如你不肯赦免孩子，那么请你赦免老人吧。"他的话是如此。可是尽管他说了千遍万遍，弥诺斯总不许他回去。知道恳求是无补于事的，他暗道："代达罗斯，一个献出你身手的机会来了。弥诺斯是陆上的主人，水上的主人，陆和水都不准我们脱逃，只剩下空间这一条路了，我是应当从那里开我的路了。统治诸天的宙斯啊，请赦我的企图。我并不敢升到你的天宫上去，可是要脱逃我的暴君，除了你的领域是没有第二条路啊。假如斯提克斯可以给我们一条路，我们早穿过斯提克斯的水了。然而既然是没路可走，我便不得不变换我的本能了。"

　　才能常常是被不幸所唤醒的。谁会相信人可以在空中旅行呢？可是代达罗斯却用翎羽来造成翼翅，用麻线缚住了，又用熔蜡胶固了底部。于是那个新的机械的工作已经完毕了。那个孩子欢乐地用手转着羽毛和蜡，不知道这个家伙是为他预备的。他的父亲对他说："这便是送我们回去的唯一的船，这是我们脱逃弥诺斯的唯一办法。他纵使断了我们一切的归路，他总不能断了我们空间的路，我们还有空间啊。用我的发明冲破那空间。可是你不可看阿尔卡狄亚的处女①和鲍沃代斯②的伴侣，把着剑的奥里雍；跟着我

■ 代达罗斯和伊卡洛斯

飞，我将飞在你前面，由我带领着，你就可平安无事了。假如在飞行的时候我们升得太高，靠近了太阳，蜡是吃不住热的；假如降得太低，靠近了大海，我们的翅便着了湿不能活动了。要飞在两者之间，而且还应当留心着风。我的儿子，你须得顺着它的方向飞去。"他一边教导，一边把翼翅缚在他的儿子身上，又教他如何拍

---

①指卡利斯托，阿耳卡狄亚王吕卡翁的女儿，被赫拉变成一头熊，宙斯将她变成大熊星座。

②星名。

动，像老鸟教小鸟一样。随后把自己的翼翅缚在肩上，胆小地飘荡在他所新开的路上。正在要飞行之前，他把他的儿子吻了许多次，而那忍不住的眼泪便在他的颊上横流着了。在那里不远有一座山岗，虽然比大山低，却统治着平原。他们便在那里开始他们冒险的脱逃。代达罗斯一边拍着翼翅，一边回头看他儿子的翼翅，可是却一点也不耽搁他的空间行程。

他们的路程的新奇已经蛊惑住他们了。不久伊卡洛斯什么恐慌也没有了，他是越飞越上劲了。一个在用细弱的芦秆钓鱼的渔夫看见了他们，把钓得的鱼也丢下了。他们已在左边过了萨摩斯、纳克索斯、帕罗斯①和为克里乌斯所爱的提洛斯②都已在他们后面了。在他们的右边已过了莱班托斯和荫着森林的加林奈和环着多鱼的水的阿斯底巴拉艾了。忽然那个太大胆的青年人很高兴地向天升上去，离开了他的父亲。他的翼翅的连接地方松了，蜡在飞近太阳时熔了，他徒劳地摇动着他的手臂，他总不能在稀薄的空中把持住身子。他在高天上恐怖地望着大海，那使他战栗的恐怖用黑暗把他的眼睛蒙住了。蜡已熔完了。他拍动着他的空空的两臂，他震颤着又

---

① 爱琴海岛名。
② 爱琴海岛名，在那里有阿波罗的神殿，克里乌斯是阿波罗的别名。

无可依托，便坠了下来。在他坠下去的时候，他高喊着："我的爸爸啊，我的爸爸啊，我被拖下来了！"当他说这话的时候，绿波把他的口掩住了。这时可怜的父亲(啊，他从此不是人父了！)喊道："伊卡洛斯！伊卡洛斯！你在哪儿，你飞在天的哪一部分？"当他已看见毛羽漂浮在海水上时，还喊着"伊卡洛斯"，大地已接受了伊卡洛斯的遗骸，大海保留着他的名字。

弥诺斯不能禁止一个凡人靠着翼翅逃走，而我却要缚住一个飞翔的神祇①！想借海蒙尼亚②的法术或是用那从小马头上割下来的东西③的人实在是大大地错误了。为要使爱情经久，美狄亚的草是没有用的，马尔西人④的毒药和魔术也全没有用的。假如魔法能维持爱情，那生在法茜丝河岸旁的公主⑤早可以留住埃宋的儿子⑥，喀耳刻⑦也早可以留住奥德修斯了。所以给少女喝春药是没有用的，春药会乱了理性而发生疯狂。

①这里指丘比特。
②海蒙尼亚是忒沙利阿的古名，那里的女子都会魔法。
③小马额上长的瘤，被视为春药。
④擅长春药及魔术的意大利古民族。
⑤指美狄亚。法茜丝是美狄亚家乡科尔喀斯的一条河。
⑥指伊阿宋，埃宋是他的父亲。
⑦仙女，爱上返乡途中的奥德修斯，但奥德修斯忠于自己的妻子，拒绝了她的诱惑。

不要用这些有罪的方法吧！你应当是可爱的，别人自然爱你了。单只有面貌或是身材的美是不够的，即使你是老荷马所赞赏的尼柔斯①或是那邪恶的水精所偷去的许拉斯②。假如你要保你的情人而无一旦被弃之虞，你应当在身体的长处上加上智慧。美是容易消残的东西：它跟着岁月一年一年地消灭下去，它不停地一年一年地坏下去。紫罗兰和百合不是永远开着花的，而蔷薇一朝凋谢后，它的空枝上只剩下刺了。你也是这样的，美丽的青年人，你的头发不久也会变白，你

■ 女巫喀耳刻施毒　沃特豪斯

① 美男子，希腊英雄。
② 美少年，在米西亚被水精偷去。

的脸上不久也会起皱纹。现在且培养你的智慧，它是经久的，而且可以做你的美的依赖，它是伴你到坟墓的唯一的瑰宝。

勤勉地去考究美术和两种语言①啊。奥德修斯并不美丽，但是他是一个善辞令的人，这已足够使两位海上的女神②为他而相思苦了。卡吕普索③多少次看见他忙着要动身而悲啼，坚决地对他说海浪不容他开船啊！她不停地要求他讲特洛伊没落的故事，那故事他换了说法不知讲过多少次了。有一天，他们在海滩上止了步，在那里，在那美丽的卡吕普索要听那奥特里赛人的首领④流血的结果。他便用那支他偶然拿在手中的轻轻的小杖为她在沙上绘起画来。他一边画着城墙，一边说："这就是特洛伊城。这是西摩伊斯⑤。譬如说我的营是在那儿。过去是一片平原（他便画一片平原），那就是我们杀死那在夜里想盗海蒙尼亚的英雄⑥的马的多隆⑦的地方。那

①希腊语和拉丁语。
②喀耳刻和卡吕普索，先后爱上奥德修斯。
③水神，俄奇吉亚岛的女王。奥德修斯在返乡的漂流途中曾经到过她的岛上。她救了遇难的奥德修斯，并爱上了他，在岛上留了他七年，才放他回家乡。
④指色雷斯国王瑞索斯，奥特里赛人就是色雷斯人。
⑤特洛伊小河。
⑥指阿喀琉斯，他生于海蒙尼亚。
⑦特洛伊的神行太保，夜晚至希腊探营时被奥德修斯杀死。

■ 许拉斯和水精们 沃特豪斯

边搭着西笃尼于斯人瑞索斯[1]的营帐；我是从那儿在夜里盗了他的马回来的。"他正要画其他的东西的时候，忽然打过一片波浪来，把特洛伊、瑞索斯的营帐和本人都带走了。于是那位女神便对他说："你还敢信赖这在你眼前抹去了如此伟名的海水取道回去吗？"因此，随便你怎样，总不要信任那欺人的美貌，要在身

---

[1] 色雷斯人，色雷斯是特洛伊盟友。有预言说，瑞索斯的马吃到特洛伊的草，希腊人就不能攻下特洛伊城。于是狄俄墨得斯和奥德修斯把他的马偷走并杀了他。

体的长处上加上别的长处。

最得人心的是那熟练的殷勤。狡猾和刁刻的话只能生人的憎恨。我们憎厌那以斗为生的鹰隼和那扑弱羊的狼，可是我们是绝对不张网捕那无害的燕子的。而在塔上，我们让那卡奥尼亚的鸟儿①自由地居住着。把那些口角和伤人的话放开得远些，爱情的食料是温柔的话。妻子离开丈夫，丈夫离开妻子都是为了口角，他们以为这样做是理所当然的。妻子的妆奁，那就是口角。至于情人呢，她是应该常常听见她所中听的话的。你们同睡在一张床上并不是法律规定的，那属于你的法律，就是爱情。你要带了温存的抚爱和多情的言语去亲近你的腻友，使她一见你去就觉得快活。

我不是为有钱的人来教爱术的，那出钱的人是用不到我的功课的。他们是用不到什么智慧的，当他要的时候，他只要说"收了这个吧"就够了。对于这种人我是只好让步的，他们的得人欢心的方法比我强得多。我这篇诗是为穷人们制的，因为我自己是穷人的时候，我曾恋爱过。当我不能送礼物的时候，我便把美丽的语言送给我的情人。穷人在爱情中应当具有深心，他应当避免一些不适当的话；他应当忍受一个有钱情人所忍受不下的许许多

----

① 指鸽子。卡奥尼亚是艾比路斯的一部分。艾比路斯有会说话的鸽子。

多的事情。我记得有一次在发怒的时候，我把我的情人的头发弄乱了，那次的发怒损失了我多少的幸福的日子啊！我不相信我撕碎了她的衫子，而且我也没有看见过，可是她却坚决地那样说，于是我不得不花钱赔她一件了。可是你们，假如你们是聪明的，就避免你们的老师的过失吧，而且也像我一样地担心着受苦痛吧。和帕提亚人去打仗；对于你的腻友呢，和平、诙谐和一切能激动爱情。

假如你的情人难服侍又对你不仁慈，你须捺着性子容受着，她不久就会柔和下去的。假如你小心地拗一根树枝，它便弯了；假如你拿起来用力一拗，它便断了。小心地顺着水流，人们便游过一条河；可是假如你逆了水性，你就总不能达到目的。人们用忍耐驯服了努米底亚的老虎和狮子，在田里的雄牛也是渐渐地屈服于犁轭的。可有比那诺那克里阿人阿塔兰忒^①更厉害的女子吗？可是随便她如何骄傲，她终究受一个男子的柔情的调理。

别人说，希波墨涅斯时常在树下哭着自己的命运和那少女的严厉，他时常受了她的命令把捕禽兽的网负在肩上，时常用他的长矛

---

① 阿尔迦地亚国王的女儿，美丽而好战，提出求婚者必须在赛跑中胜过她。美少年希波墨涅斯边跑边扔下象征天下最美的金苹果，阿塔兰忒忙于捡苹果，输给了希波墨涅斯，只好嫁给了他。

■ 阿塔兰忒和希波墨涅斯　雷尼

去刺那可怕的野猪。他甚至中了希拉曷斯[1]的箭，可是别支箭[2]他也是受过的啊！我并不命令你手里拿着兵器到梅拿鲁斯山的森林中去，也不命令你把沉重的网背在肩上，我更不命令你去袒露受箭。聪明人，我的课程将给你最容易学的命令。

---

① 半人半马怪，被阿塔兰忒杀死。
② 指爱神丘比特的金箭。

假如你的情人不依你，那么你便让步，让步后才会得到胜利。不论她叫你去做什么事，你总需为她做好。她所骂的，你也骂；她所称赞的，你也称赞。她要说的，你也说；她所否认的，你也否认着。她假如笑，你陪着她笑；她假如哭，你也少不得流泪。一言以蔽之，你要照着她的脸色来定自己的脸色。

她喜欢博弈，她的手掷着象牙骰子，你呢，要故意掷得不好，然后把骰子递给她。假如玩小骨牌游戏，为要不使她因为失败而悲伤，你总应当要让她赢；假如棋盘是你们的战场，你的玻璃棋子也应当被你的敌手打败的。

■ 赫拉克勒斯和翁法勒　勒姆瓦那

你须得为她打着遮阳伞；假如她挤在人群中，你便为她开路；你要匆匆地走到踏脚板边去扶她上床；将鞋儿脱下或者穿上她的双足。而且往往即使你自己也很冷，你也得把你的情人的冻冷的手暖在你怀里。用你的手，自由人的手，去为她拿着镜子，这虽然有点不好意思，但绝对不要害羞。

那个使母亲倦于把怪物放在他路上的神祇，那注定进那他起初背过的天堂的神祇，说曾经在伊奥尼阿的处女们间拿过女红篮又纺过羊毛。梯林斯的英雄①都服从他的腻友的命令。你现在不要踌躇，快去忍受他所忍受过的吧！

假如她约你到市场去相会，你须得常常在约定时间前老早等在那里，而回来却越晚越好。她对你说："你到某处来。"你便将一切事情都放去了跑去，不使群众延迟了你的步履。当在晚间，她从华筵里出来，叫一个奴隶领路回去的时候，你立刻自荐上去。她在乡间写信给你说："请即惠临。"丘比特是憎恨迟慢的，没有车儿，你便立刻拔起脚来上路。什么都不能阻拦你，天气不好也不管，炙热的大暑也不管，大雪铺了满街也不管。

爱情是一种军中的服役。懦怯的人们，退后吧，懦夫是不配保护这些旗帜的。幽夜、寒冬、远路、辛楚、烦劳，这全是在这快乐的战场上所须忍受的。你须得时常忍受那云片注在你身上的雨水，你又须得时常忍着寒冷，着地而睡。别人说，肯丢斯的神祇②放牧阿德墨托斯国王的牛的时候，他只有一间小茅屋作栖身处。阿波罗

---

① 赫拉克勒斯。
② 指阿波罗，他出生在肯丢斯山。

都不以为害羞的事谁会当作可耻？丢掉一切的骄傲吧，假如你要恋爱长久。假如你没有一条安全又容易的路去会你的情人，假如门关得紧紧的，不能使你进去，好，你便爬上屋顶去，由这条险路到你情人那里去；或者从高窗上溜进去也可以。她知道了你的冒险的缘故一定会非常高兴，这就是你的爱情的确实的保证。利安得①啊，你可以不必常常去看你的情人；你破浪游过海水，向她证实你的情感。

不应当以和侍女、女佣、奴隶结交为可耻。向他们一个个地致敬，这是于你无损的。你要去握他们的微贱的手。而且，在福耳图纳的日子②，你还得送些小礼给那些向你讨礼物的奴隶，这在你是所费有限的。而在迦里阿人受了罗马的侍女们的衣饰所骗而丧生的日子③，也送点礼物给侍女。相信我，把这些小人物都搜罗在你自己的利益中，不要忘了那守门人和看守卧房的门的奴隶。

我也并不叫你拿华美的礼物去送你的情人，送她些不值什么钱的东西，只要是精选而送得适宜就是了。在田野铺陈着它的富庶的时候，当果树垂实累累的时候，差一个奴隶送一满篮的乡村礼物给

① 美少年，爱上了维纳斯的女祭司海洛，冒大风浪游泳去会海洛，溺死。
② 6月24日，罗马第六个国王为命运女神福耳图纳建立神殿的日子。
③ 7月7日，是女仆节，这一天，女仆们打败了罗马的敌人。

她。虽然果子不过是从圣路①上买来的,你却可以对她说是从乡间采来的。送她些葡萄或是艾玛瑞里斯②所爱吃的栗子③。可是今日的艾玛瑞里斯是不很爱吃栗子了。你甚至还可以送她一只画眉鸟或是一个花鬘④,表示你是在思念着她。我知道别人也有买这些东西去送没有儿女的老人,冀望在他死后得他的遗产。啊!拿这些礼物来做那种不怀好意的用途的人简直该死!我可要劝你赠她几首情诗吗?啊啊!诗词并不是体面的。她们赞美诗词,但是她们却要的是贵重的礼物:只要有钱,即使是一个粗人也得人欢心的。我们的时代真正是黄金时代⑤,用黄金,我们得到最大的荣誉;用黄金,我们使恋爱顺利。是的,荷马啊,即使你伴着九位缪斯回来,假如你双手空空,一无所有,荷马啊,别人准会把你赶出门去。虽然有学识的女子并不是没有,可是总在少数;旁的女子却是什么也不懂的,却要混充渊博。可是你作起诗来,却须二者都得称颂的。而你的诗,不管好不好,总要说得中听,使人觉得有价值。不论她们是有学问的

---

① 圣路上有果子铺。
② 田园诗歌中的美丽牧女。
③ 维吉尔《牧歌》第二章:"我亲自采了那有柔毛的白色野木瓜,和我的艾玛瑞里斯所爱的栗子。"
④ 戴在身上作装饰的花环。
⑤ 第一代人类的时代,他们有着神一样的生活,也有着神一样的美德。

■ 接受花冠的情人 弗拉戈纳尔

或没学问的，那首费了一夜没有睡而为她们所作的诗，对她们总抵得上一点小礼物的效力。

尤其是当你决定去做一些你以为是有用的事的时候，你总要想法引你的情人来请你去做。假如你要把自由给予你的奴隶，你应当使她来请求你给予他；假如你要饶赦一个应受刑罚的奴隶，也要使她请求你去做。你尽收着实利，面子却尽让给她：你一点也没有损失的，而她却自以为她对你很有权威了。

可是假如你存心要保持你的情人的爱情，你须做出那使她相信你是在惊赏她的美的样子。她披戴一袭蒂路斯①的绛色的大氅，你便夸称那袭蒂路斯的绛色大氅。她穿着一件高斯的织物，你便说高斯②的织物她穿起来最配。她闪耀着金饰，你便对她说在你看来黄金还不及她的娇容灿烂。假如她穿着重袭，你便称赞那件袭衣。假如她穿着一件单衫，你便高呼起来："你使我眼睛都看花了！"一面低微地请求她当心，不要冻坏了身子。假如她的发丝是艺术地分开在额前，你便称赞这种梳法；假如她的头发是用热铁卷过的，你便应该说："好美丽的鬈发！"在她跳舞的时候，赞叹她的声音；而当她停息了的时

①腓尼基的一个地名，出产绛色染料。
②爱琴海中的一个岛。

候，你便自怨自艾地说完得太快了。待她允许你和她同睡之后，你便可以崇拜那使你幸福的东西了，你便可以用一种快乐得战栗的声音表示出你的狂欢来。

是的，即使她比可怕的美杜莎①还凶，她也会为她的情郎变成温柔而容易服侍的。你尤其应当善于矫饰，使她不能察觉，而你的脸上千万不能露出你的言语来。艺术隐藏着是有用的，显露出来便成为羞耻，而且永远失去了别人的信心了。

时常，在快到秋天的时候，正是一年间最好的时节。那时，葡

---

① 蛇发妖女，后为珀耳修斯所杀。

萄累累地垂着；那时，我们感到一阵透骨的新寒，有时感到一阵炙人的炎热，这种天气的不正常是容易使我们疲倦的。愿你的情人在那时很健康！可是有些微恙把她牵制在床上，假如她受天气不好的影响而生病，那便是你显示出你的爱情和你忠心的时候了，那便是应当播种以得一个丰富的收获的时候了。

你要不怕烦琐地去侍候她的病；你的手需要去做一切她所委任的事；要使她看见你哭泣；不要不和她去亲嘴，要使她枯干的嘴唇饮着你的眼泪！为她的健康许愿，应答尤其是要高声；而且要时常预备着些吉兆的梦去对她讲。叫一个老妇拿着硫黄和赎罪的蛋去清洁她的床。在她的心里，这些辛劳会永远地留着一个温柔的记忆。多少人用这种方法去在遗嘱上得到一个地位啊！可是当心着，太讨好是要惹起病人的讨厌的。你的多情的勋劳须得要有一个限制。禁止她吃闲食和请她吃苦药等事情你是不应当去做的！这些事让你的敌人去做。

可是那当你离开港口的时候的风，不就是当你航行在大海中的时候和你合宜的风！爱情在初生的时候是微弱的，它将由习惯而坚强起来。

你需得好好地养育它，它便慢慢地坚强了。这头你现在畏惧的雄牛，在它小的时候你曾抚摩过；这株你在它荫下高卧的大树，起初不过是一根小小的枝儿。

江河是涓滴而成的。设法使你的美人和你熟稔，因为唯有习惯最有力量。为了得到她的心，切莫在任何敌人前面退却。要使她不断地看见你，要使她不断地听见你的声音。日间、夜间，你须得常常在她眼前。可是当你坚决地相信她能念念不忘你的时候，你便离开她，要使你的离别给予她一些牵挂。给她一些休息，一片休息过的田种起来是愈加丰盛的，一片干燥的土吸起雨水来是愈加猛烈的。菲利斯①当得摩丰在她身边的时候，她的爱情是并不十分热烈的，一等他航海去后，她的情焰却高烧起来了。珀涅罗珀因为聪明的奥德修斯的别离而痛苦；而你的眼泪，拉俄达弥亚②啊，将那费拉古斯的孙子③喊回来。

可是，为谨慎起见，你的别离总以短一些为是，时间会减弱牵记之心。长久看不见的情郎是容易被遗忘的，别人将取而代之了。

---

① 色雷斯国王西同的女儿，忒修斯之子得摩丰的未婚妻。得摩丰没有按时迎娶她，她竟自缢而死。
② 普洛忒西拉俄斯的妻子。传说她丈夫死后，她的哭声感动众神，于是答应让她丈夫复活三个小时。三小时后，她自杀在丈夫的怀抱中。
③ 指普洛忒西拉俄斯，特洛伊战争中第一个进入特洛伊城的希腊人，被赫克托耳所杀。

■ 帕里斯与海伦 大卫

墨涅拉俄斯不在家的时候，海伦忍不住孤眠的滋味，便到她的宾客①
的怀中去温存了。墨涅拉俄斯，你是多么的傻啊！你独自个走了，
把你的妻子和你的宾客放在一个屋子里。傻子！这简直是把温柔的

———————

① 指帕里斯。

鸽子放在老鹰的爪子里，把柔羊托付给饥饿的血口！不，海伦是一点也没有罪，她的情夫也一点没有罪。他做了你自己或是随便哪一个可以做的事。那是你强迫他们成奸的，供给了他们时间和地点。这可不仿佛是你自己叫你的年轻的妻子这样做的吗？她做什么呢？她的丈夫不在家；在她旁边是一个并不粗蠢的宾客，而且她又是生怕孤眠的。请阿特柔斯的儿子①想一想他要怎样吧。我是宽恕海伦的，她不过利用一个多情的丈夫的殷勤而已。可是，那正被猎人放出猎犬去追的时候的狂怒的野猪，那正在哺乳给小狮子吃的母狮，那旅人不小心踏着的蝮蛇，都没有一个在丈夫的床上捉住情敌的女子那样的可怕。她的狂怒活画在她的脸上，铁器、火，在她一切都是好的；她忘记了一切的节制，她跑着，像被阿沃尼亚的神祇②的角所触动的跳神诸女一样。丈夫的罪恶，结发夫妻的背誓，一个生在法茜丝河畔的野蛮的妻子③在她自己的儿子身上报复了。另一个变了本性的母亲呢，那就是这只你所看见的燕子。你看着它，它胸口还染着鲜血。那最适当的配偶，最坚固的关系便是这样断裂的，一个聪明的男子不应当去煽起这种妒忌的暴怒。

---

① 指墨涅拉俄斯。
② 指巴克斯，他的角力大无穷。
③ 指美狄亚。

■ 克吕泰墨斯特拉和情夫埃癸斯托斯谋杀阿伽门农

严苛的批评者啊，我并不判定你只准有一个情人。天保佑我！一个已结婚的女子是很难守着这种约束的。娱乐吧，可是须得谨慎；你的多情的窃食须要暗藏着，不应该夸耀出来。不要拿一件另一个女子可以认得出来的礼物送给一个女子；改变你们的幽会的地点和时间，莫使一个女子知道了你的秘密来揭穿你。当你写信的时候，在未寄之前须细细地重看一遍，许多情人都能看得出弦外之音来。被冒犯了的维纳斯拿起了武器，来一箭，还一箭，使那放箭的人也受到苦痛。当阿特柔斯的儿子①满意他的妻子②的时候她是贞洁的，她丈夫的薄幸使她犯了罪。她知道了那个手里拿着月桂冠、额上缠着圣带的克律塞斯③不能收回自己的女儿了。她知道了，利尔奈索斯的女子④，那引起你的痛苦又经过可耻的迟延而延长战争的掠劫。这些她不过是耳闻罢了，可是那普里阿摩斯的女儿⑤，她是亲眼看见的，因为，真可羞，那个胜利者反倒做了他的俘虏的俘虏了。从此那廷达瑞俄斯的女儿⑥便让梯厄斯忒斯的儿子⑦投到她心中，投到她床上了。她用一种罪恶去报复她丈夫的罪恶。

假如你的行为，虽则隐藏得很好，一朝忽然露了出来，或者竟是被发觉出来，你须得要否认到底。不要比平常更卑屈、更谄媚些，因为这就是贼胆心虚的表示。你须要用尽平生的力，用那对

---

① 指阿特柔斯之子阿伽门农。
② 指克吕泰墨斯特拉。
③ 阿波罗神的一个祭司。
④ 指布里塞伊斯，利尔奈索斯是她的出生地，特洛伊的一个镇。
⑤ 指卡珊德拉，被阿伽门农掠为女奴。
⑥ 指克吕泰墨斯特拉。
⑦ 指埃癸斯托斯。

于情战的全盘的精力。和平只有这样才换得到，应当用眠床来证明你以前没有偷尝过维纳斯的幽欢过的。有些老妇劝你用玉帚那种恶草，或是胡椒伴着刺激的荨麻子，或是黄虫菊浸陈酒来做兴奋剂，在我看来，这些简直是毒药。那住在艾里克斯山①的幽阴的山风中的女神，是不愿用这些人工的方法来激起她们的欢乐的。那你可以用的，是从希腊阿尔加都思②的城运到我们这儿来的白胡葱，是生在我们的园子里的动情的草，是鸡蛋，是叙美托斯③的蜜，是松球包着的松子。

可是多才的埃拉托啊，你为什么使我迷途在这些邪术中？回到我的车子所不能越出的正路吧。刚才我劝你隐藏你的薄幸，现在我却劝你换一条路走，表现出你的薄幸来。不要骂我矛盾！船并不是每阵风都适宜的。它航行在波上，有时被从脱拉喀阿来的北风推动着，有时被东南风推动着，温暖的西风和南风轮流地送着它的帆。你看那车上的御人吧：有时他放松了缰绳，有时他勒住了那狂奔的马。

有些女子是不喜欢怯懦的顺从的，没有一个情敌，她们的爱情

---

① 西西里岛中的一座山名，那有一座有名的维纳斯庙。
② 珀罗普斯之子，希腊的美迦拉城的重建者；此处指美迦拉城。
③ 非洲的一座山名，以蜜蜂及云石出名。

■ 宙斯与赫拉　阿尼巴·卡拉齐
——妒忌的赫拉常因宙斯的好色而愤怒不已。

是要消歇下去的。幸福时常使我们沉醉，但是人们却难久享着它。火没有了燃料便渐渐地暗熄下去，消隐在白白的灰底。可是一撒上硫黄，那好像是沉睡了过去的火便重新燃烧而放出一道新的光芒来。因此，假如一颗心憔悴在一种无知觉的麻痹中，你便应用嫉妒的针去刺它醒来。你须要使你的情人为你而不安宁，唤醒她冷去的心的热焰，使她知道你的薄幸而脸儿发青。哦，哪有一个自觉受了欺凌而啜泣的情人，是一百倍、一千倍的幸福啊！那她还愿意怀疑的他的犯罪的消息一传到她耳边，她就晕过去了，不幸的女子啊！她脸儿和声音同时都变了。我是多么愿意做那被她在暴怒中拔着头发的人啊！我是多么愿意做那被她用指甲抓破脸儿又使她看了落泪的人啊！她怒看着这个人，没有了他，她是不能活的，但是她是愿意活的！可是你要问我了，我应当让她失望多少时候呢？

我将回答你：时间不可长，否则她的怒气就要有力了。赶快用你的手臂缠住她的玉颈，将她涕泪淋漓的脸儿紧贴在你的胸口。把密吻给予她的眼泪，将维纳斯的幽欢给予她的眼泪。这样便和平无事了。这是息怒的唯一的方法。可是当她怒不可遏时，当她对你不肯甘休时，你便请求她在床上签订和平公约，她便柔和下去了。要不用武力而安处在和议厅中正是这样的，相信我，宽恕是从那个地方产生出来的。那些刚才相争过的鸽子亲起嘴来格外有情，而它们的鸣声是一种爱情的语言。

宇宙起初不过是一团混沌，其中也不分天、地和水。不久天升到地面上，而海又环围着陆地，而空虚的混沌便变成各种的原型了。树林便做了野兽的居所，空间成了飞鸟的家乡，游鱼则潜藏

在水底。那时人类孤寂地漂泊在田野间，他们只是有力而无智，只是个粗蛮的身体。他们以树林为屋，以野草为食，以树叶为床；他们很长久地互相不认识。别人说，那柔化了他们的蛮性的是使男子和女子合在一张床上的温柔的逸乐。他们要做的事情，他们单独地自己学会了，也用不到请教先生。维纳斯也不用艺术帮忙，竟完成了她的温柔的公干。鸟儿有它所爱的雌鸟，鱼儿在水中找到一个伴儿来平分它的欢乐。雌鹿跟随着雄鹿，蛇和蛇合在一起，雄狗和雌狗配对。母羊和母牛沉醉在公羊和公牛的抚爱中。那雄山羊，随它如何不洁，也不使放荡的雌山羊扫兴。在爱情的狂热中的母马，甚至会越过河流到远处去找雄马。

　　勇敢啊！用这些强有力的药去平息你情妇的怒，这种药能使她在深切的苦痛中睡去；这比马卡翁一切的液汁都灵验，假如你有过失，只有它能够使你得到宽恕。

　　我的歌的题旨是这样，忽然阿波罗现身在我前面，他用手指拨着他的金琴，一枝月桂在他手中；一个月桂冠戴在他头上。他用一种先知的态度和口气向我说："放逸的爱情的大师，快把你的弟子们领到我的殿中来吧。他们在那儿可以念那全世界闻名的铭文：'凡人，认识你自己。'只有那认识自己的人在他的爱情中会聪明，只有他会量力而行。假如老天赐予他一副俏脸儿，他应该要知道去利用它；假如他有一身好皮肤，他须得时常袒肩而卧；假如他话说得很漂亮，便不可默默地一声也不响。他假如善唱，就应该唱；善饮，就应该饮。可是烦琐的演说家和怪癖的诗人啊，千万不要朗诵你们的散文或是诗来打断谈话。"福玻斯的教言是如此。有情的人们啊，服从福玻斯的高论吧！你们可以完全信任这从神明的口中发出来的言语。可是我的题旨在呼唤我了。凡是谨慎地爱着又听从我的艺术的教条的人，总一定会胜利而达到他的目的。

田不常有好收成，风也不常帮助舟人。欢乐很少而悲痛却很多，这就是多情的男子们的命运。愿他准备着那灵魂去受千万的折磨吧。阿托斯山①上的兔子，希勃拉山②上的蜜蜂，荫密的萜拉丝树③上的珠果，海滩上的贝壳，这些比起恋爱的痛苦来真是少极

---

① 迦尔喀斯半岛上的一座山。
② 西西里岛的一座山，山上的蜜蜂很有名。
③ 指橄榄树。

了。我们所中的箭上是满蘸着苦胆的。正当你看见你的情人是在家的时候，他们却会对你说她已经出去了。有什么要紧，算她已出去，你的眼睛看错就是了。她允许你在夜间见她，而到了夜间她的门却关得紧紧的。忍受着，睡在肮脏的地上。或者有个欺谎的侍女前来粗蛮地向你说："这人为什么拦在我们门前？"那时你便当恳求这忍心的侍女，甚至那闭着的门，又把那在你头上的蔷薇①放在门槛上。假如你的情人愿意见你，你便跑进去；假如她拒绝你，你便应当跑了。一个有教养的人是不应该做引人憎厌的人的。你难道要你的情人说"简直没有方法避免这个可厌的人"吗？

美人儿总是恩怨无常的。不要怕羞去受她的辱骂，挨她的打，或是去吻她的纤足。

可是，我为什么要说到这样琐细的地方去呢？我们且注力于重

------

① 因为他是从筵席上回来，所以戴着蔷薇花冠。蔷薇放在门槛上是求爱的表示。

要的题目吧。我要唱重大的事项了。老百姓，请当心着啊，我的企图是冒险的，可是没有冒险，哪里会有成功？我的功课所要求你的是一件繁难的工作。耐心地忍受着一个情敌，你的凯旋才靠得住，你才可以得胜进入宙斯的神殿。相信我，这并不是凡夫的俗见，却是希腊的橡树①的神示。这是我所授的艺术的无上的教条。

假如你的情人向你的情敌做眉眼、打手势，你要忍受着。她写信给他，你切莫去碰一碰她的信，听她自由地来来去去。多少的丈夫以这种殷勤对他们的发妻，尤其是当一觉好梦来帮助瞒过他们的时候！至于我，我承认我是不能达到完善的地步。怎么办呢？我还够不到我的艺术。什么！在我眼前，假如有人向我的美人眉眼传情起来，我便痛苦得了不得，我忍不住要生气了！我记得有一天有人和她接了一个吻，我便攻击这一吻，我们的爱情充满了无理的诛求！而这个毛病在女人身旁伤害我不知多少次。最老练的人是允许别人到他情人那儿去。最好是装聋作哑，什么也不知道，让她掩藏着她的不忠，不然，久之她脸也不会红一红了。年轻的多情人啊，千万不要去揭穿你们的情人。让她们欺骗你们，让她们在欺骗你们的时候以为你们是受她们好话的骗的。揭穿一对情人，那一对情人

---

① 指艾比路斯的道道尼阿的橡树，据说会启示神意。

■ 因爱而结合的维纳斯和马尔斯 委罗内塞

的爱情反而愈深了。等到他们两个利害相关的时候，他们便坚持到底以偿他们的损失了。

有一个故事是全奥林匹亚①都知道的：就是伏尔甘②用狡计当场拿获马尔斯和维纳斯的故事。那马尔斯神狂爱着维纳斯。这凶猛的战士便变成一个柔顺的情人了。维纳斯对他也不生疏，也不残忍，她的心比任何女神都温柔。别人说，那个热恋着的女子多少次嘲笑着她的丈夫的跛行和他的被火或是被工作所弄硬的手！同时，她在马尔斯的面前学起伏尔甘的样子来：这样在他看来是娇媚极了，而她的讽

———————

① 众神的居处。
② 罗马神话中的火神，维纳斯的丈夫。

刺的风姿更使她的美加高千倍。他们起初还只是偷偷摸摸地爱着，他们的热情是掩藏着而且是害羞的。可是太阳（谁能逃过太阳的眼睛呢？）却向伏尔甘揭露出他的妻子的行为来。你给了一个多么不如意的例子啊，太阳！你不如去向维纳斯去请赏吧。对于你的守着沉默，她总会给你些东西做代价的。伏尔甘在床的四周和上边布着些穿不透的网罗，这是眼睛所不能看见的。然后他假装动身到利姆诺斯①去。这一对情人便来幽会了，于是双双地、赤条条地被捕在网中了。

伏尔甘召请诸神，将这捉住的一对情人给他们看。别人说，维纳斯是几乎眼泪也忍不住了。这两个情人既不能遮他们的脸，又不能用手蔽住那不可见人的地方。那时有一个神祇笑着说了："诸神中最勇敢的马尔斯，假如铁链弄得你不舒服，把它们让给我吧。"后来尼普顿请求伏尔甘，他才放了这两个因犯。马尔斯避到脱拉喀阿②去，维纳斯避到帕福斯③去。

伏尔甘，依你说这于你有什么好处呢？不久之前他们还掩藏着他们的爱情，现在却公开出来了，因为他们已打破一切的羞耻了。

---

① 希腊地名，那里的人崇拜伏尔甘。
② 马尔斯的居处。
③ 那里的人崇拜维纳斯。

■ 遭到伏尔甘突然袭击的维纳斯和马尔斯　布歇
　——伏尔甘抓住偷情的维纳斯和马尔斯的情景。

你常常承认你的行为是愚笨而鲁莽，而且别人说你是正忏悔着你自己的谋划。我不许你设计陷人，那被丈夫当场拿获的狄俄涅也禁止你设那种她曾受过苦来的陷阱。

不要布罗网去害你的情敌，不要去盗秘密的情书。就是要做，也得让她的正式丈夫去做。至于我，我重新再申说一遍，我这儿所唱的只是法律所不禁的幽欢。我们不要把任何贵妇混到我们的游戏中来。

谁敢将刻瑞斯①的圣祭和在萨莫色雷斯②独创的庄严的教仪揭露给教外人看呢？守秘密是一件微小的功德。反之，说出一件不应当说的事来却是一个大大的罪过。不谨慎的坦塔罗斯③不能取得那悬在他头上的果子，又在水中渴得要死，那简直是活该。维纳斯尤其禁止别人揭穿她的秘密，我警告你，任何多言的人都不准走近她的祭坛去。维纳斯的供养并不是藏在柜中的，献祭的时候钟也不是连连地敲着的，我们大家都可以参与，这有一个条件，就是大家都需守秘密。就是维纳斯自己，当她卸了衣裳的时候，她也用手把她的

---

① 罗马的农事女神。
② 爱琴海上的一个岛。
③ 吕狄亚国王，因为泄露诸神的秘密，被放在一个湖的中央，水一直浸到他颈边，但他要喝水时，水就退了开去。他头上垂挂着极好的果子，但他要去吃时，果子就被风吹到云端。

秘密的销魂处遮住。牲畜的交尾是到处可以看到的，人人可以看到的；可是少女们即使已经看见了，总避而不看。

我们的幽会所不可少的是一间闭得很紧的房间，而且把我们的不可示人的东西用布遮住。假如我们不要幽暗，至少也要半晦或是比白昼暗一些。在那还没有瓦来遮蔽太阳和雨的时代，在那以橡树来做荫蔽做食料的时代，多情的人们不在光天化日之下，而在山洞里和林底里偷尝爱情的美味。那种野蛮的时代已经重视羞耻了！可是现在我们却标榜着我们的夜间的功绩，我们以高价换得的是什么呢？讲它出来是唯一的快乐，而且在到处细说着一切女子的爱娇。要碰到一个人就说："这个女子我也曾结识过。"要时常有一个女子可以指点给别人看，要使一切你想染指的女子都成了轻佻的谈话的目标。这还不算数，有些人造出些故事来（这些故事假如是真的他们准会否认了），听他们的话，他们是得到了一切女子的恩眷的。假如他们不能接触她们的身体，他们能够坏她们的名声；身体虽然贞洁，而名誉却坏了。可憎的守卒，现在请你滚开吧，把你的情妇关起来，门上加着重重的闩锁。对于这些自欺地夸耀着说已得到了她其实不能到手的幸福的人，这些防范有什么用呢？

至于我们呢，我们只含蓄地讲着我们的真实的成功；我们的偷香窃玉是受一种不可穿透的缄默的神秘所保护着的。

你尤其是不可以对一个女子指摘出她的坏处：多少的情人们都是装聋作哑地过去！安德洛墨达① 的脸的颜色，那每只脚上有一双翼翅的人② 是从来不批评的。安德洛玛刻③ 的身材是大众认为过高的：只有一个人认为修长合度，他就是赫克托耳。你所不爱看的应该去看惯，你便很容易受得下去了；习惯成为自然，而初生的爱

---

① 相传她的肤色是棕色的。
② 指珀耳修斯。
③ 赫克托耳之妻。

■ 向安德洛玛刻告别的赫克特耳 考芙曼

情却是什么也注意到的。这开始在绿色的树皮中滋育着的嫩枝，假如微风一吹，它就要折断了，可是不久跟着时间牢固起来，它甚至能和风抵抗，而且结出果子来了。时间消灭一切，即使是那体形的丑陋，而那我们觉得不完美的，久而久之也不成为不完善的了。在没有习惯的时候，我们的鼻子是受不住牛皮的气味的，久而久之鼻子闻惯了，便不觉得讨厌了。而且还有许多字眼可以用来掩饰那些坏处。那皮肤比伊利里亚的松脂还要黑的女子，你可以说她是浅棕色。她的眼睛是斜的呢？你可以比她作维纳斯。她的眼睛是黄色的呢？你说这是雅典娜的颜色。那瘦得似乎只有奄奄一息的，你就说是体态轻盈。矮小的就说是娇小玲珑，肥大的就说是盛态丰肌。总而言之，用最相近的品格来掩饰那些坏处。

不要向她问年纪，更不要打听她的出身。让督察官去施行他的责任吧，尤其当她已不在青春的芳年中了，良时已过，而她已在拔她的灰白的头发的时候。青年人啊，这个年龄，或者甚至是更老一点的年龄，并不是没有用的。是啊，这片别人所轻视的田却有收成；是啊，这片田是宜于播种的。

努力啊，当你的气力和你的青春可以对付的时候；不久那使你佝偻的衰年就要悄悄来临了。用你的桨劈开海水，或是用你的犁分开泥土，或是用你的孔武有力的手拿着杀人的武器，或是用你的男子的精力和你的殷勤去供奉女人。这最后的一种也是一种军队服役，这最后一种也能得到利益的。

加之这些女人对于爱情的工作都十分渊博，而且她们都是有经验的，因为只有经验造成艺术家。她们用化妆盖去了时间的损害，又小心地不露出老妇人的样子来。她会体贴你的心情，做出许多姿态来，随便哪一集秘戏图都没有比她多变化。在她身上，幽欢不是

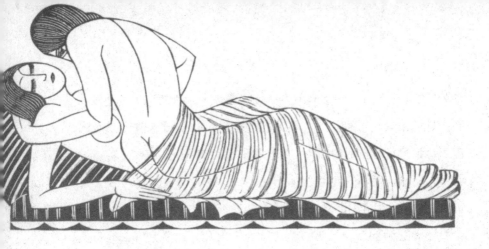

由人工的激动而生出来的，那真正温柔的幽欢是应当男子和女子都有份的。

我恨那些不是两方同样热烈的拥抱（这就是我爱少女觉得兴味很少的缘故）。我恨那些"应该"委身过来而委身过来的女子，她一点也感觉不到什么，还在想着她的纺锤。那种因为是本分而允许我的欢乐，在我是不成为欢乐的。我不要一个女子对我有什么本分。我愿意听见她那泄露出她所感受到的欢乐的声音，和恳求我延长她的幸福的声音。我爱看她沉醉着逸乐，懒洋洋地凝看着我；或是憔悴着爱情，长久地不愿人去碰她一碰。可是这种利益，老天是不赐予青年人的，要到中年才能遇到。性急的人去喝新酒吧，我呢，你倒那一直从前任执政官时代就盛在一个双杯中的我们的祖先所酿的陈酒给我们喝吧。槲树要经过许多岁月才能抵抗阿波罗的光，而那新割过的草地却伤了我们的脚。什么！在赫耳弥俄涅和海伦之间你宁愿要赫耳弥俄涅吗？而高尔葛①又胜过她的母亲吗？总之，你要尝成熟的爱情的果子，只要你不固执，你总会如愿以偿的。

现在那个从犯——床——已接受了我们的一对有情人了。缪斯啊，在他们的卧室的闭着的门前止步吧。没有你，他们也很会找出许多的话来的，而且在床上他们的手是不会有空闲的。他们的手指也会在丘比特喜欢把他的箭射过去的神秘的地方去找事情做的。从前那最英武的赫克托耳是如此的对付安德洛玛刻的，赫克托耳所擅长的并不只是打仗。那伟大的阿喀琉斯也是如此地对付他的利尔奈索斯的女俘虏②的，当他战乏了，睡在一张柔软的床上的时候。布里塞伊斯啊，你一点也不畏惧地受着那双常染着特洛伊人的血的手的抚爱。陶醉的美人啊，那时你所最爱的，可不正是感到那胜利者的手紧搂着你那回事吗？相信我，不要太急于达到那陶醉的境地，你须得要经过许多次的迟延，不知不觉地达到那境地。当你已找到了一个女子所最受抚爱的地方，你须得不怕羞去抚爱。于是你会看见你的情人的眼睛里闪着一道颤动的光，像水波所反射出来的太阳光一样。随后是一阵夹着甜蜜的低语的怨语声，醉人的呻吟，和那

———————————

① 阿尔泰娅之女。
② 指布里塞伊斯。

兴奋起爱情的蜜语。可是你不要把帆张得太满而把你的情人剩在后面，也不要让她走在你前面。目的地是要同时达到的。当男子和女子两个都同时战败了，一点没有气力地瘫着，那正是无上的欢乐啊！当你悠闲自在的时候和没有恐怖来催你匆匆了事的时候，这就是你应该遵照的规则，可是当延迟会发生危险的时候，那时你便弯身在桨上竭力地划着，而且用刺马轮刺着你的骏马。

我的大著快要结束了。感恩的青年人啊，给我棕榈，而且在我的熏香的发上给我戴一个石榴花冠。犹如包达里虑斯①在希腊人中以医术出名；阿喀琉斯以武勇出名，涅斯托耳②以机警出名；犹如卡尔卡斯③之于占卜，忒拉蒙④的儿子之于统兵，奥托墨冬之于驾车；我呢，我的精于爱术亦如此。

　　多情的男子，歌颂你们的诗人啊，使我的姓氏为全世界所歌唱。我把武器供给你们，伏尔甘把武器供给阿喀琉斯⑤；愿我的礼品给你们胜利，正如阿喀琉斯得到胜利一样。而且我希望凡是用我所赠的剑的人们战胜了一个亚马逊人⑥之后，在他们的战利品上这样写：

　　"奥维德是我的老师。"

　　可是现在那些多情的少女们前来向我求教了。年轻的美人儿，为了你们，我才遗下后面的诗章。

---

　　①医药神埃斯科拉庇俄斯之子，希腊名医。
　　②特洛伊战争中，希腊一方最有经验的人。
　　③希腊军中的占卜者。
　　④希腊英雄大埃阿斯之父。
　　⑤阿喀琉斯的好友帕特洛克罗斯借了阿喀琉斯的甲和盾去和赫克托耳作战，被赫克托耳所杀。阿喀琉斯听见挚友已死，甲盾丧失，既悲且怒。他的母亲为他求天上的铁匠伏尔甘为他一夜造成甲胄兵器，后来终于杀死了赫克托耳。
　　⑥强悍的女子民族，生了男孩都扔掉，并烧去左乳以便射箭。

第三卷

爱情的良方

On Winning and Holding Love

我刚才武装起希腊人来战亚马逊人，彭忒西勒亚①啊，现在我要拿武器给你和你的骁勇的军队了。用相等的武器去上阵吧，胜利是属于维纳斯和张着翼翅飞遍全宇宙的孩子②所宠幸的人。让你们一无防御地受着那武装得很好的敌人的攻击是不应该的，而在你呢，男子，这样战胜了也是可羞的。

可是或许有一个人要说了："你为什么还要拿新的毒液给蝮蛇啊？你为什么要把羊棚打开让凶猛的雌狼进来啊？"请你们不要把几个女人的罪加到一切女子的身上去，我们应该照她们各人的行为来作判断。阿特柔斯的幼子和长子③可以提出一个严重的责备，一个是对于海伦的，一个是对于海伦的姐姐④的；达拉奥思⑤的女儿厄里费勒⑥的罪，活活地将骑着活马的奥伊克葛斯的儿子赶到斯提克斯河岸⑦上去。

但是珀涅罗珀当她的丈夫十年征战、十年漂泊的时间守着贞

---

① 亚马逊人的女王，特洛伊人的同盟，被阿喀琉斯杀死。
② 指丘比特。
③ 指墨涅拉俄斯和阿伽门农。
④ 指克吕泰墨斯特拉。
⑤ 乘阿尔戈船远征者之一。
⑥ 安菲阿拉俄斯之妻，受贿主张丈夫忒拜，致使安菲阿拉俄斯陷入地中而死。奥伊克葛斯的儿子是指安菲阿拉俄斯。
⑦ 指冥土。

■ 珀涅罗珀与她的求婚者们 沃特豪斯

——正在纺织的珀涅罗珀毫不愿应付各种求婚者的打扰，咬在唇边的一丝黑线，表达出她的坚定，始终坚守她的贞节。

节。请想想那费拉古斯的孙子①和那在如花的年纪追陪他到黄泉中的人②吧。

巴加沙的女子③用了自己的生命把她的丈夫——斐瑞斯的儿子④

———————

① 指普洛忒西拉俄斯。
② 指拉俄达弥亚。
③ 指阿尔刻斯提，代丈夫去死，后被赫拉克勒斯从冥间带回。
④ 指阿德墨托斯，斐瑞斯是他的父亲。

的生命重买回来。"接受我呀，卡帕纽斯①，我们的骨灰至少要合在一起的。"伊菲阿斯②说着，便纵身跳到焚尸场中去。

德行是以女子为衣，以女子为名的，她受它的恩宠难道是可诧异的吗？然而我的艺术却不是教这些伟大的灵魂的，我的船只要较小一点的帆就够了。我只教授轻飘的爱情，我将教女人如何会惹人怜爱。女人不懂得抵抗丘比特的火和利箭，我觉得他的箭穿入女子的心比穿入男子的心更深。男子们是老欺人的，纤弱的女人们欺人的却不多。你且把女性来研究一下吧，你就会发现负心的是很少的。那已做了母亲的生在法茜丝岸上的女子③，受了伊阿宋的欺骗和抛弃，那伊阿宋在怀间接受了另一个新娘④。忒修斯啊，阿里阿德涅独自个被弃在她所不认识的地方，几乎做了海鸟的食料。你去考察一下为什么有一条路叫"九条路"，回答是：树林哭泣着菲利斯，把它们的叶子落在她的坟上。你的宾客是虔信人的名誉的，然而，艾丽莎⑤啊，你从他那儿接受到一把剑和失望，便自杀了。不幸的

---

① 攻忒拜七英雄之一。其妻欧阿德涅。她跳入骨灰内，以身殉夫。
② 欧阿德涅，伊菲斯之女，卡帕纽斯之妻。
③ 指美狄亚。
④ 指克莱乌莎。
⑤ 狄多，迦太基女王。她爱上特洛伊亡命的英雄埃涅阿斯，但后来埃涅阿斯按照神意离去，她便自杀。

人们啊，我将告诉你们的惨遇的原因：你们不懂得恋爱。你们缺少艺术，而那使爱情持久的正是艺术。

就是到今日她们仍旧不懂得，可是那塞西拉的女神①命我把我的课程去教女子。她现身在我面前对我说："那些不幸的女子有什么得罪了你吗？你将她们那些没有抵抗力的队伍投到武装得很好的男子们那儿去。那些男子，你已为他们著了两卷书，已把他们的爱术教得精通了，女性自然也轮到接受你的功课了。那起初贬骂那生在忒拉泊奈的妻子的人②，随后在一篇更幸福的诗中歌颂她③了。假如我认识曾经爱过女人们的你，请你不要叫她们吃亏吧。这个服务的报偿，你一生之中都可以要求的。"当她站在我前

---

①指维纳斯。
②指古希腊诗人斯特西科罗斯。
③指海伦。

■ 狄安娜与恩底弥翁 焦尔达诺

面的时候这样说着，又从那戴在她头上的石榴冠上，摘下了一片叶子和几粒石榴给我。当我接受的时候，我感着一个神明的感应，空气是格外光辉而清净，而工作的疲倦又绝对不压在我心上了。当维纳斯感兴起我的时候，女子啊！到这里来求学吧！贞节和法律都准许你，你的利益也在邀请你。

从今以后请你想一想那不久将来到的衰老吧：这样你便不会把流光虚掷了。当你还能玩的时候，当你还在生命的春日的时候，娱乐啊！年华如逝水一样地流去了，逝波是永不会回到水源的，时光一朝过去，也一样地去而不返。不要辜负了好时光：它如此快地飞去了，今日是总不如昨日好的。在这些荆棘丛生的地方，我曾经看见紫罗兰漫开过，这枝生刺的荆棘从前曾经供给过我很好的花冠。

你现在年纪还轻，推开了你的情郎，可是当有一个时候来到了，衰老又孤单，你夜间将在孤冷的床上战栗着了。你的门不会被情敌们的夜间的争执所打破，而且在早晨，你更不会看见在门槛上铺满了蔷薇。啊啊！我们的皮肤是那样快地起皱了！我们的灿烂的容颜是那样快地改变了！那你发誓说你做少女时就有的白发不就要满头了？蛇蜕了皮就蜕掉了它的衰老，鹿换了角便又变作年轻了，可是时间从我们那儿夺去的长处是什么都不能补救的。花开堪折直须折，莫待无花空折枝啊。多生孩子是格外能使人老得快的，收获的次数太多会把田弄枯。"月"啊，恩底弥翁[1]在拉特摩斯山上没有使你害羞，而刻法罗斯[2]之被蔷薇手指的女神[3]所抢得是没有什么可羞的，而阿多尼斯更是不用说了，维纳斯到现在还哭着他。她的

---

[1] 俊美的牧人，月神狄安娜爱上他，她把他带到拉特摩斯山上，恐怕他老去变丑，设法使他永远熟睡。

[2] 年轻的猎人，奥罗拉爱上他，将他抢了去，但他始终忠于自己的妻子普洛克里斯。

[3] 指黎明女神奥罗拉。

埃涅阿斯和哈耳摩尼亚①是从哪儿来的呢？凡女啊，你们须学着神仙的榜样，不要拒绝你们的情郎所希望的，你们可以给他们那些欢乐。

假设他们欺骗了你们，你们会损失些什么呢？你们所有的一切，你们仍旧保留着。一千个人可以得到你们的恩宠，可是他们不能损失你万一。工夫久了，铁石都会磨穿；可是我所说的那件东西却能抵抗一切，你也用不到怕有丝毫损失。一支蜡烛在接一个火给别一支蜡烛的时候会失去光亮吗？小小的一勺会枯了沧海吗？可是，或许有一个女子回答男子说："没有法子。"什么？你会损失什么？不过是你拿来洗浴的水吧。我并不是劝你委身于一切过路人的，不过请求你不要怀疑有什么损失吧。在你赐予的时候，你是一无损失的。

不久，我是要一阵更有力的风了，现在我还在港口，一阵轻风已足够送我前进了！

我先从冶容之术开始。栽培得好好的葡萄能得多量的酒，耕耘得好好的田收获就丰富。美貌是天赐的礼物，可是能以美貌来骄傲的有几个？你们之中有许多人都没有接受到这种赐予。冶容之术会给你一张俊俏的脸儿。一张脸儿假使不事修饰，即使它是像伊达良

---

① 埃涅阿斯是维纳斯和安喀塞斯的儿子，哈耳摩尼亚是维纳斯和马尔斯的女儿。

■ 奥罗拉和刻法罗斯 皮埃尔-纳西斯

的女神①的脸儿一样，也会失去它的一切光彩。假如从前的女子们不关心冶容，那么她们的丈夫也不会关心她们了。假如那披在安德洛玛刻身上的衫子是粗布做的，可值得诧异吗？她的丈夫②不过是一个粗鲁的兵。有人可看见阿瑞斯的妻子装束得很华美地去见她的以七张牛皮做盾的丈夫吗？

从前一种乡村的纯朴统治着，现在的罗马却璀璨着黄金又拥有它所征服的全世界的浩瀚的财富。你且看看现在的加比都良③和从前的加比都良吧，人们会说这是供奉另一个宙斯的了。元老院现在很配那庄严的集会。在达丢斯王④治国的时候，它不过是一所简单的茅舍而已。这巴拉丁山，在那里有阿波罗和我们的领袖们保护之下的灿烂的大厦，在那时是什么呢？一片耕牛的牧场而已。让别人去夸耀往昔吧，我呢，我是自庆生在今世的。现在这世纪是合我的脾胃的。这可是因为在今日人们从地下采取黄金，人们从各处海岸上采取珠贝，人们看见山因采取大理石而消灭下去，和我们的大坝把青色的波涛打退了吗？不是的，是因为现在人们讲究冶容之术，

————————————

① 指维纳斯。伊达良的人们崇奉维纳斯。
② 指赫克托耳。
③ 供奉宙斯的神殿。
④ 萨宾族的王。

104

而长久留在我们祖先时候
的鄙野，到我们这时候已
不存在了。

可是，你们却也不要
把那些黑色的印度人在绿
水里采来的高价的宝石挂在
耳上，也不要披着那妨碍你
们的轻盈的、坠着黄金的锦
衣。这种场面，你们本来
是想用来引诱我们的，结
果却反将我们吓跑了。

素雅的装束才会使你

■ 照镜子的维纳斯　提香

惹人怜爱。不要把你们的头发弄乱，梳头妈妈的手能够增加美丽或
是减损美丽。梳头有许许多多的式样，每人选择一个适合自己的式
样，第一要紧的就是要照一照镜子。脸儿长的须得将头发分梳在额
上，不用什么装饰，这就是拉俄达弥亚的梳法；把头发梳起来，在
额前梳成一个小髻，让耳朵露出来，这种梳法宜于圆脸的女子；有
的少妇让长发披拂在肩头，和谐的阿波罗啊，正像你一样，当你在
调琴时；有的却应该梳起辫子，像那老是穿着短短的衫子在林中追

逐猛兽时的狄安娜一样；有的飘着卷曲的头发使我们着迷；有的把头发梳得平平的，贴在鬓边，使我们销魂。有的应该簪着玳瑁的梳子做装饰；有的应该把头发卷着波纹。浓密的橡树的橡实、希勃拉山的蜜蜂、阿尔贝山①的野兽都可以计算，而每日出来的梳头的新花样却数也数不清。随便的梳妆有许多人是相配的，这种梳妆别人以为是前一日梳了现在重新整理一下的。艺术应该模仿偶然。在破城后，伊俄勒②现身于赫拉克勒斯面前的时候也是这个模样的。赫拉克勒斯一见她就说："我所爱的正是这个人。"而你，被弃的纳克索斯地方的女儿③，当你在萨提洛斯们的"曷荷艾"呼声中被巴克斯举到他的车上的时候，你也是这个模样的。

　　女人啊，老天对于你们的爱娇是多么的肯出力帮忙，你们有千种的方法来补救时间的损害。至于我们男子呢，我们简直没有方法去掩盖时间的损害。我们的被年岁带去的头发，像被北风所吹落的树叶一样地凋落。女人呢，用格尔马奈④的草汁来染她们的白发。技术给予她们一种假借的颜色，比天然的颜色更好看。女人呢，装

---

① 欧洲西南部山脉。
② 俄卡利亚国王的女儿。
③ 指阿里阿德涅。
④ 格尔马奈人用草染发。

着她刚买来的茸厚的头发走向前来，而且，只要花几个钱，别人的发就变了她们的了。而且她们是公然在赫拉克勒斯和缪斯们面前买假发也不害羞的。

■ 罗马妇女的装扮

关于衣饰我说些什么呢？那种华丽的镶边和用蒂路斯红染过的毛织物和我有什么关系呢？价值便宜些的颜色正多着！为什么要把你全部的财产全背在身上呢？你看这天蓝，正像被南风吹散了雨云的晴天一样。你看这金黄，这正是从伊诺①的毒计中救出佛里克索斯和赫勒来的公羊的颜色。这绿色模仿着海水，由海水而得到它的名称。我很愿意相信这是水上仙子的衫子。这个颜色像郁金草，就是那沾着露水驾着光耀

---

① 阿塔玛斯后妻。她想将阿塔玛斯前妻涅斐勒的孩子佛里克索斯和赫勒弄死。但赫耳墨斯给了赫勒一头金毛的公羊，她把自己的子女放在羊背上，便从伊诺的手中逃脱出来，但赫勒不幸中途坠海。

■ 珀尔修斯和安德洛墨达 莱顿

的骏马的女神① 的郁金草衫子的颜色。那里你可以找到巴福斯的番石榴的颜色，这里有紫红宝石色、苍白的蔷薇色或是脱拉岂阿的鹤羽色。我们还有艾玛瑞里斯啊，你所爱吃的栗子的颜色、杏仁的颜色和从蜜蜡得到名称的布的颜色。毛织物所染的颜色，是和那春天的温息使葡萄抽芽又驱逐了那闲懒的冬天的时候地上所发的花枝的颜色一样多，也许还更多些。

在这许多颜色之间，你留意选择吧！因为一切颜色不是都适合于一切女子的。黑色是配合皮肤皎白的女子的，黑色是适合于布里塞伊斯的，当她被掠的时候，她正穿着黑色的衣裳。白色是宜于棕色的女子的，刻甫斯的女儿② 啊，一件白色的衫子使你变成格外娇

---

① 指奥罗拉，黎明之女神。
② 指埃塞俄比亚公主安德洛墨达。

媚，这就是你降落到赛里福斯岛①时所穿的衣裳的颜色。

我正要告诉你不要使你腋下有狐臭，不要使你的腿上矗起粗毛。可是我的功课并不是教授那些住在高加索山岩下的女子和喝着米西亚的加伊古司河水的女子的。叫你们不要疏忽把牙齿弄干净和每天早晨在梳妆台上洗净了脸有什么用呢？你们会用铅粉来涂白你们的脸儿，皮肤天生不娇红的人可以用人工使它红的。你们的艺术还能补救眉毛离得太开的毛病，又能用"颜妆"贴住你们年龄的痕迹。你们更不要害羞去用细灰或是生在澄清的启特诺斯河岸上的郁金草染在眼圈上来增加你们眼睛的光彩。关于那些使你美丽的方法，我已著有专论②，虽然是短短的，却很精密重要。不被老天所宠幸的青年女子，你们亦可以到那儿去讨救兵，我的艺术是不吝以有益的话来教你们的。

可是不要使你的情郎瞥见你摊满了小盒子坐在桌旁，要让艺术使你美丽而不给别人看见。看见那酒滓儿满涂在你们的脸上，因重而坠下来流到你胸口，谁会不厌恶呢？那以脂质液来做原料的粉的气味是那样的一种气味啊！虽然这液体是从没有洗过的羊毛中取

---

① 爱琴海中的一个岛。
② 指奥维德的《论冶容》。

出，从雅典运来的。我更不劝你在别人面前用鹿髓，或是在别人的面前净牙齿。这些我很知道是能使你格外娇媚，可是那种光景却是不很体面的。多少事情在做的时候是何等的难看，而当做好之后却使我们看了何等的喜欢！今天你们看看这些雕像，勤苦的米洛①的杰作，在从前不过是一块顽石，一块不成形的金属。要做一个金戒指是先要捶金的，你现在所穿的衣裳从前只是一些不干净的羊毛。这大理石像，从前只是一块不成东西的石头，而现在已成为著名的雕像，这是在绞去头发上的水的裸体的维纳斯②。同样，当你们在你们的美上用功夫的时候，你们让我们以为你们还睡着吧。待你们妆成后出来，好处就多了。为什么要我知道你们的脸儿皎白的原因呢？把你们卧室的门关起来吧。为什么要把那不完全的工程显露出来呢？有许许多多事情男子们是应该朦胧的。假使内幕被我们看穿了，差不多什么外表都会受我们厌恶的。戏场上金色的饰物，你仔细去看看，那不过是一块木头上包了一层薄薄的金叶子罢了！戏不演完时是不准看客走近去看的。因此你们应当在男子们不在旁边的时候妆扮，这是同样的理由。

---

① 希腊著名雕刻家。
② 指米洛的作品《出水的维纳斯》。

■ 勒达与天鹅 达·芬奇

然而我却并不禁止你们在我们面前叫人梳理头发：我爱看你们的发丝披拂在你们的肩头。可是你应当没有一切坏性子，又不可叫人几次三番地拆了又梳，梳了又拆。不要使你们的梳头妈妈对于你们有所恐惧。我恨那些用指甲抓破梳头妈妈的脸和用发针刺她的手臂的女人们。她诅咒着她的女主人的头，那她还捧在手上的头，同时，她流着血把她的泪滴到那可恶的头发上。

一切不能夸耀自己的头发的女子应得在门旁放一个步哨，或者老是在善良女神①庙里去梳头。有一天，他们向一个女子通报我的突然的光临，在匆忙之中，她把假发都装倒了。愿这样大的侮辱加在我们的仇敌的身上去吧！愿这种耻辱留给帕提亚②的女子吧！一只牛没有角，一片地没有草，一株树没有叶和一个头没有发都是极丑的东西。

塞墨勒③或是勒达④啊，我的课程并不是教你们的，被一头假牛所载到海外的西顿的女子⑤啊，我的课程也不是教你的，更不是教海伦的。这海伦，墨涅拉俄斯啊，你索取她是理应正当的；而你，抢她

---

① 罗马女人所崇奉的司生殖的女神，她的神庙是禁止男子入内的。
② 罗马人的宿敌。
③ 大地女神，为宙斯所爱，和他生了巴克斯。
④ 斯巴达王廷达瑞俄斯之妻。宙斯爱上了她，变成一头白鹅去亲近她，和她生了子女。
⑤ 指欧罗巴，因为她是腓尼基国王的女儿，西顿是腓尼基最古老的城。

的特洛伊人啊，你不放她亦是有理由的。

我的女弟子群中美的丑的都有，而丑的尤其占大多数！美的女子不必一定要我的功课的帮助和教训，她们有那属于她们的美，并不需

■ 抢夺欧罗巴 布歇

要艺术来施行它的权威。当大海平静的时候，舵工是可以平安地休息的；起了风浪的时候，他便不离开他的舵了。可是一张没有缺点的脸儿是很少的！藏过这些缺点，而且，尽力地减少你身体上的不完善。假如你较矮的，你便坐着，因为怕你站着的时候使人还以为你是坐着；假如你是矮子，你便当躺在床上。这样躺着，别人便打量不出你的身材了。更用一件衫子把你的脚遮住。太瘦小，你便穿厚布的衣服，再用一件很大的大氅披在肩上。惨白的脸便须搽上胭脂，棕色的脸便得向鳄鱼①讨救兵。畸形的脚须得藏在精细的白皮

---

① 古罗马的妇女从鳄鱼腹中取出白色来敷面。

113

鞋里；干瘦的腿切莫不裹皮带露出来给人看见。薄薄的小垫子补救了肩头的高低不齐；假如胸脯扁平的，便得遮一块胸袜。假如你的手指太粗或是你的指甲太粗糙，说话的时候千万不可做手势。口气太重的女子，在肚子饿的时候切不可说话，而且对男子说话的时候也应站得远远的。假如你的牙齿太黑，太长，太不整齐，那么你一笑就大糟而特糟了。

谁会相信呢？女子甚至还学习如何笑，这艺术能使她们格外爱娇。口不要开得太大，要使你的颊上起两个小小的酒窝儿，使下唇盖住上面的牙尖。笑的时候不要太长久，笑的次数不要太多，这样你的笑就温柔、细腻，人人爱听了。有的女子扭曲了她们的嘴大笑，做出怪难看的样子；有的女子大声地笑着，我们听起来却像是在哭着。还有一些女子拿那粗蠢而不愉快的声音来乱我们的耳朵，正像那牵磨的老母驴子鸣声一样。

艺术哪一处不伸张到啊？女子甚至还学习哭得好看呢！她们流着眼泪，在她们要哭或者好像要哭的时候。

那些吃去了重要的字母和勉强使她的舌头格格不吐的女人我又怎样说呢？这种读音的毛病在她们是一种爱娇：她们学习着说得更不好些。

这是琐细的事，可是既然是有用的，你便得当心研究。你们须学着和女子适合的步法。在步履中有一种不可忽视的美，它能够吸引或是推开一个你所不认识的男子。这一个，臀部摆动得合法，使她的长衫随风摇曳，尊贵地一步步地向前走去。那一个，像一个翁布里①的村夫的黄面婆一样，跨着大步走着。关于这一点，正如和其他事件一样，应当有个节度。这一个太乡下气了，那一个太柔软太小心了。而且，你须得让肩头和左臂的上部露出来。这事对于皮肤雪白的女人尤其合宜。被这种光景所激动，我会渴望去吻着我从那肩头所见的一切。

塞壬②是海上的妖精，她们用那悦耳的歌声把飞驶的船弄停了。西绪福斯的儿子③听了她们的歌声，几乎要把那缚他的绳子弄断，而他的同伴们，幸亏那封住耳朵的蜡，才没有被诱惑。悦耳的歌声是一种迷人的东西：女子啊，学着唱歌吧（有许多面貌不美丽的女子是用声音来做诱惑的方法的）。你们应当有时背诵着那你们从云石的剧场里听来的曲子，有时唱着那带着特有的节奏的尼罗河的轻歌。那些要向我来求教的女子们不应该不懂得用右手握胡弓，

---

① 意大利的一个民族。
② 一种鸟形而生着妇人的头的海上怪物，以歌声迷乱水手，使其罹难。
③ 指奥德修斯，他的母亲被暴君西绪福斯强奸。

■ 吸引动物的俄耳甫斯 布歇

左手拿箜篌的艺术。罗多彼山①的歌人俄耳甫斯②能用他的琴韵去感动岩石、猛兽、鞑靼的湖和三头犬。你这个很正当的替母亲去复仇的人③啊，听了你的歌声，那些顽石很听话地前来搭成一座新的城墙了。鱼虽然是哑的，却会感受琴韵，假如你相信那大众咸知的阿里昂④的故事。更学着用两手挥弹古琴吧：这个欢快的乐器是利于爱情的。

你们还须得知道卡利马科斯⑤、高斯的诗人⑥和戴奥斯的老人⑦——酒的朋友的诗歌。你们也得认识了萨福⑧（还有什么东西比她的诗更妖艳多情吗？）和那个写一个被那欺诈的葛达所骗的父亲的米南德的诗。你也可以念念那多情的普罗佩提乌斯⑨、几章

---

① 色雷斯的山名。
② 色雷斯吟游诗人。
③ 指忒拜国王安菲翁。他的母亲安提俄珀被她的堂位的叔婶虐待致死，安菲翁率军攻陷忒拜，为母复仇。安菲翁善奏琴，琴声能使石子自己聚拢来，围成一座墙。
④ 7世纪的希腊诗人和琴手。他航海被劫，被投入海中，用音乐引来一头海豚救了他。
⑤ 公元前4世纪希腊诗人。
⑥ 指菲勒塔斯，高斯人，希腊诗人忒俄克里托斯的老师。
⑦ 指阿那克里翁（公元前560—前478），希腊诗人，生于戴奥斯。
⑧ 希腊女诗人。
⑨ 公元前1世纪罗马诗人。

加鲁斯①的或是我们那可爱的提布鲁斯②的诗，或是瓦罗③所制的咏那佛里克索斯的妹妹和那如此不幸的金毛公羊的诗。你们尤其应当念念那咏流亡的埃涅阿斯——崇高的罗马的建设者的行旅的诗人④的诗，这是拉丁族的最大的杰作。

或许鄙人的贱名也可以附骥于他们的鸿名之下。或许拙作不会被莱带河⑤的水所淹没。是的，或许有一个人会说："假如你真是一个有学问的女子，你念念那我们的老师开导男女两性的诗章⑥。或者在他所作的题名为《爱情》的三卷诗章中，选几节你将用温柔又清脆的声音来念的诗吧。或者，用一种轻盈的声调来念他的《名人书简》的一篇吧，这种体裁在他以前是没有人知道的，他是发明者。"

阿波罗，强有力的生角的巴克斯，还有你们，贞洁的姊妹们，诗人的保护的神衹⑦，请垂听我的愿心啊！

---

① 罗马诗人和雄辩家。
② 罗马诗人，生于公元前54年，死于公元前19年（？）。
③ 罗马诗人和作家。
④ 指维尔吉及其名作《埃涅阿斯》。
⑤ 冥土中的一条河，饮其水者忘记过去的一切，"被莱带河的水所淹没"是被人遗忘了的意思。
⑥ 指本书。
⑦ 指九位缪斯神。

■ 萨福、法翁和小爱神 大卫

　　我希望——这个别人是无可怀疑的——女子能够跳舞。这样，当别人请求她跳舞的时候，她可以走过筵席来，优美地摆动着她的手臂。好的跳舞家使剧场中看客皆大欢喜。这种优美的艺术在我们是多么的有诱惑力啊！

　　我很惭愧说得这样琐细，可是我希望我的门徒能精于掷骰子，而且一掷下去就会算出点数来。她应该有时掷出三点，有时恰巧掷出那可以赢的和所需要的点数来。我也希望我的门徒下起棋来不要吃败仗。一个"卒"是打不过两个敌人的，"王"是须得和"后"分离着打仗的，一拼命，敌人就逃了。火气把我们的性格暴露出来，而我们的心情也被人赤裸裸地看穿了。生气、赢钱心占住了我们，因此便发生吵嘴、打架和苦痛的遗憾。我们互相埋怨了，口角声在空气里都布满了，每个人宣着神号相骂了。在赌里，信用是没有的，为要赢钱，人们是什么愿心也许下了！我甚至时常看见那些满脸流着眼泪的人。想求爱的女子们，愿宙斯神为你们免了这些可耻的短处吧！

女子啊，这些就是你们优雅的天性所允许你们的玩意儿。在男子们呢，他们的范围更大了。他们的玩意儿有网球、标枪、铁饼、武器和练马。体育场是不合你们的口味的，处女泉^①的冰冷的水也和你们不合宜，都斯古斯的平静的河水^②中，你们也不会去的。那你们可以的，而且在你们是有用的，就是在"太阳"的骏马跑进"处女宫"的时候^③，到庞培门下去散散步，到巴拉丁山上的戴月桂冠的

---

① 在罗马体育场中，赛过车或角过力的人，都到那里去洗去灰尘和汗水。泉水很冷。
② 指谛勃里斯河。
③ 指8月。

■ 恺撒把克利奥佩特拉扶上王位

阿波罗的神殿里去巡礼一番——那在海底里把巴莱多尼恩① 人的兵船
弄沉的就是他——或者到那"大帝"的妹妹和皇后，和他的戴海军王
冠的女婿所建筑的纪念物边去走走也好②。那为孟斐斯的母牛③ 献着

————————————

　　① 埃及沿海的一个城。此处指在亚克兴的战役，在那场战役中奥古斯都打败了
安东尼和埃及艳后克利奥佩特拉。古埃及最后一代君主，艳后克利奥佩特拉，是一个
靠情爱维持统治的君王。她利用美貌和魅力倾倒了罗马的将军们，先后让恺撒大帝及
安东尼将军拜倒在她的石榴裙下。
　　② "大帝"指奥古斯都，妹妹是屋大维娅，皇后是利维亚，女婿是马库斯·阿
格里帕。
　　③ 指伊希斯。

香烛的神坛下也要去。那可以出风头的三个戏院①尤其不可不去。那新血还热着的竞技场和转着飞奔的马车的赛车场也得常去跑跑。

隐掩者终不为人所知；不为人所知者不为人所欲。一张妍丽的脸儿，假如不给别人看，那还有什么用呢？你唱，你便可以超过达米拉斯②和阿默勃斯③。你的琴韵，假如不为别人所听得，如何能得大名呢？假如那高斯的画家阿佩利斯④不把他的"维纳斯画"出展，这位女神恐怕到现在还沉没在大海里吧。

除了"不朽"，那些诗人的野心是什么呢？这是我们的工作所等着的最后的目的。在从前，诗人是为神祇和国王所宠爱的，在古代，他们的歌是能够得到无数报偿的。诗人的名字是神圣而受人尊敬的，而且人们往往给他们无数的财富。伟大的西庇阿⑤啊，那生在卡拉布里亚半岛的山间的恩尼乌斯⑥是被人认为陪葬在你旁边的。可是现在是斯文扫地了，对于缪斯们的勤劳也得到了一个"游

---

① 指巴尔步斯剧场、马尔凯卢斯剧场和庞培剧场。
② 色雷斯的诗人。
③ 雅典最有名的演员。
④ 画家，生于高斯岛。他画了一幅名画《出水的维纳斯》，奥古斯都将这幅画藏在恺撒的庙堂里。日久画毁，尼禄王代之以道罗德斯所作《维纳斯像》。其时阿佩利斯重为高斯岛人绘维纳斯像，较前作更胜十倍，但未竣而阿佩利斯已死。
⑤ 罗马大将。
⑥ 罗马诗人，罗马史诗的创制者。

手好闲"的名称了。可是无论如何我们总是喜欢刻苦求名的。谁会认识荷马呢？假如那部不朽的杰作《伊利亚特》到如今还不为人所知。谁会认识达娜厄①呢？假如她老是深居在她的塔中。她一定无人知晓，而变作一个老太婆了。

■ 达娜厄 伦勃朗

　　青年的美人们啊，凑热闹是有用的。你们须得时常跑到外边去。雌狼是到大群绵羊里去找食料的，宙斯的鸟是在多小鸟的田间翱翔着的，美丽的女子也应该在群众间露脸。在大群的人中，她或许可以找到一个可以诱惑的男子。她须得到处搔首弄姿，还须得注意能增加美好的一切。机会是到处都有的，老是把持着你们的钓钩吧，在那你以为没有什么鱼的水里会有鱼的。猎狗在多树木的山上

---

　　① 阿克瑞斯之女，被父亲幽闭在塔中，宙斯变成金雨，冲破了塔得到了她，生珀耳修斯。

到处搜寻而一无所得是常事，而人们并不打猎，麋鹿却会自己投到罗网中来。那被绑在岩石上的安德洛墨达所能希望的最后的事，可不就是看见自己的眼泪诱惑什么人吗？在自己丈夫埋葬的时候找到另一个男子是常有的事。披头散发地走着，又让自己眼泪流着，这在女人是再好看也没有了。

可是对那些炫弄服饰和漂亮的，每根头发都有自己的一定位置的男子们，你们是应该置之不理的。他们所对你们说的话，他们是早已向千千万万的女子说过了的，他们的爱情是绝对靠不住的。一个女子，对于一个比自己还无恒，比自己还多情的男子，有什么办法呢？这事你是不会相信的，可是你应该信服我。普里阿摩斯的女儿[①]啊，假如听了你的话，特洛伊城恐怕到现在也不会攻破呢。有些男人戴着爱情的假面具向女子来钻营，他们只想从这条路去找些不自然的获得。不要被他们用松脂油涂得亮光光的头发，或是紧束着腰带的华服，或是那些满戴在手指上的指环所诱惑了去。或许那穿得最漂亮的竟会是一个贼，想偷你的华丽的衣饰。"把我们的东西还我啊！"这就是被骗的女子们时常喊着的。整个公堂都震响着这种呼声：

"把我的东西还我啊！"维纳斯啊，你的邻女们阿比阿斯啊，

---

①指卡珊德拉。

你们一点也不感动地从你们的金碧辉煌的庙上看着这些纠葛。除了那些窃贼以外，还有那些著名的淫棍，上了他们的当的女人，便免不得分担他们的恶名。前车可鉴，你们的门永不应该让一个诱惑者进来。刻克洛普斯的女儿

■ 家神维斯太

们① 啊，不要相信忒修斯的誓言，他凭神祇发誓这不是第一次啊。而你，得摩丰，忒修斯的薄幸的承嗣者，在欺骗过菲利斯以后，已没有人相信你了。

假如你们的情人满口说得很好听，你们也像他们一样地满口说得很好听就是了。假如他们拿东西送你们，你们也用相当的情谊回答他们，一个女子是能够熄灭维斯太②的永远的火，掠取伊纳古斯③的女儿的神祠里的圣物，献毒酒给丈夫喝的，假如收了情夫的礼物

① 指雅典女子。
② 罗马家神。
③ 河神，伊俄的父亲。

而不把爱的狂欢给他。

可是我不愈说愈远了。缪斯，勒住你的骏马吧，不要越出范围。一个简帖前来探测了，一个伶俐的侍女收下它了，当心地念着它，信上所用的语气是足够使你辨得出那些所表白的心愿是否真诚的，是否出于迷恋着的心的。

不要立刻就复信。等待，只要是不太长久，是能够把爱情弄得格外热烈的。对于一个年轻的情郎的请求，你须得要搭些架子，可是也不要一口回绝。要弄得他心惊胆跳，同时也要给他些希望，减少他的害怕。女子们所用的词句应当简洁而亲切：平常谈话的口气是再可爱也没有了。多少次啊，一封信燃起了一颗心的游移的情焰！多少次啊，一种不通的词句毁坏了美的幻影！

可是，既然不带那贞洁的假面具，要欺骗你们的丈夫而不使他们起疑，你们便须得要有一个谨慎的侍女或是奴隶来为你们传书递简。年轻而没有经验的奴仆是万万靠不住的。无疑的，那个保守着这种把柄的人是没有良心的，可是他所有的兵器是比埃特纳山① 的雷霆还厉害啊。我看见过无数的女子，为了这种的不谨慎，害怕到脸儿发青，吃尽一辈子的大亏。

_____

① 意大利火山，传说是宙斯的雷电工场。

126

在我想来，我们可以用欺骗答欺骗，而法律也允许以兵器攻兵器的，你们须得要有一只手写出几种笔迹来的本领。（啊！那些使我逼不得已教你们采取这种方法的人们给我死了吧！）不先把字迹擦去而复信的人真是傻子，简帖儿上是留着两个人的手迹了。当你们作书给你们的情郎的时候，你须得用那写给女友的口气，在你的信上，要称"他"的地方都须得称"她"。

可是我们且把这些琐事按下不提而说那重要事情。为要保持你们的颜面好看，你们须得把你们的脾气忍住不发出来。心平气和是合于人类的，正如暴怒是合于猛兽的一样。一发怒，脸儿便板起了，黑血把脉络也涨粗了，而在眼睛里，戈耳工的一切的火都燃起来了。"走开，你这可恶的笛子；我不值得为你牺牲我的美。"帕拉斯在水里看见了自己的影子①便这样说。你们也如此，在你们盛怒的时候，假如你们去照一照镜子，恐怕没有一个人会认得出那是你们的脸儿来。骄傲也会破坏你们的美丽，要勾起爱情，是要媚眼儿的。相信我的经验吧；太骄傲的神气我们是憎厌的。往往虽说一句话也不说，脸上也带着恨的根苗的。

有人注视你，你也注视他。有人向你温柔地微笑，你也向他温

_____

① 笛子是帕拉斯（即雅典娜）发明的，但是当她在水中照见自己吹笛时缩着嘴唇的样子，便立刻把笛子丢了。

■ 哀悼赫克托耳死亡的安德洛玛刻 大卫

柔地微笑。假如有人向你点头,你也向他打个招呼。丘比特也是先用钝箭尝试,然后从箭囊里拔出利箭来的。

我们亦憎厌悲哀。让黛克梅莎去被阿约斯①所爱吧,像我们这种快乐的民族,一个快乐的女子才能勾动起我们的春心。不,绝对不是安德洛玛刻,绝对不是黛克梅莎,你们两人中,我一个也不想你们来做我的情人。我甚至还不大相信,虽则你们的子孙使我不得不相信,你们曾和你们的丈夫同床过。一个沉浸在悲哀中的女人,怎样会对埃阿斯说"我的生命啊"和一切在男子们听了要全身舒畅的话呢?

请你们允许我对于我的无足轻重的艺术来引用几个伟大的艺术的例子,而且请你们允许我把这艺术和总兵的大元帅的企图来比拟。一位精明的大元帅把一百个步兵的统带权托付给一个将官,把一队骑兵托付给另一个将官,把旗卫兵托付给又一个将官。你们也是如此,你们须得审察一下,我们中某人做某事是相配的,是对于你们有用的。要有钱的人送礼物,要法学家出主意,要律师打官司,我们这些作诗的人呢,要我们作诗送你们。

我们这一群诗人比什么人都多懂些恋爱;我们会使那叫我们迷

---

① 埃阿斯之妻。

■ 诗人和缪斯

恋的美人闻名遐迩。涅墨西斯① 是出名了，辛西娅② 也出名了。自西至东，丽高里斯③ 的名字谁都知道了，而且人们也时常问起那我所讴歌的科琳娜④ 是谁。我还要说，那些诗人，神圣的人物，是有一颗不知道"负心"的心，而我们的艺术又用它的意象把我们改造过了。我们是既不为野心，又不为金钱所动摇的。我们厌恶名利，只要阴暗和一张卧榻就满足了。我们是容易结识的，我们是烧着一堆长久而热烈的情火的，我们是知道用真心真意爱着的。无疑的，我们的性格已经受我们的和平的艺术陶冶过了，而我们的习惯也是和我们的努力同化了。

青年的美人啊，对于诗人们，鲍艾沃帝阿的神祇⑤ 的弟子，你

① 古罗马诗人提布鲁斯（约公元前54—前19）诗中所歌咏的人。
② 古罗马诗人普罗佩提乌斯（约公元前50—前15）诗中所歌咏的人。
③ 古罗马诗人卡图鲁斯（约公元前87—前54）诗中所歌咏的人。
④ 奥维德诗中所歌咏的人，见《爱情》。
⑤ 指缪斯，因为缪斯们的居处赫利孔山是在鲍艾沃帝阿。

们是应当迁就些的。灵风使他们有利，缪斯宠爱他们，我们身上附着神明，而我们又和天有交往，我们的灵感是从天上降下来的。博学的诗人等待金钱是一种罪恶。啊啊！这一种什么女子都怕做的罪恶。女人啊，你们至少要会矫饰，不要一下子就把你们的贪心露出来。一看见是陷阱，一个新的情郎就要吓跑了。

一个老练的马夫的用辔，对于新马和对于旧马是不相同的。同一的理由，为要引诱一颗有经验的心和一个青春的少年，你们是不应该取同样的方法的。

那个你准许进你的卧房里去的，第一次进情场的新手，新的猎品，是应该使他只知道你，是应该使他老是在你的旁边，这是应该四旁围着篱笆的植物。你需要担心情敌：只要你伴着他不放松，你就一定胜利了。维纳斯的权，正如国王的权一样，是一离开就糟的。

至于那别一个，那个老兵，是会神不知鬼不觉地，乖乖地爱着的。他能忍下许多新兵所忍受不下的事情。他不会打破你们的门或是烧你们的门。他不会用他的指甲抓破了他的情人的嫩脸，他不会撕破她的长衣或是一个女子的衫子，而且，在他，马被劫去了也不会流眼泪的。

那激情是一个在青春期和恋爱期中的少年所仅有的。而别一个呢，他会耐心地忍受着那些最厉害的伤楚。他所燃烧着的情火是

■ 爱的譬喻:尊敬 委罗内塞

不旺的，啊啊！正如燃烧着湿草，或是新从山上砍下来的柴一样。这种的爱情是靠得住的，而那种激动的爱情虽是热烈，但是不能经久。快些去采那一现的昙花啊。

我就要把一切献给我们的敌人①了（我们早就开门临敌了），而对于我的叛逆，我也是存着至诚不欺之心。太容易垂青是难长久养育爱情的，在温柔的欢乐中应该夹入些拒绝。让你们的情郎留在

---

① 指女子。

门口，要使他叫着"忍心的门"，要使他不停地哀求和威吓。清淡的东西我们是不喜欢的，一种苦的饮料倒能打开我们的胃口。一只船被顺风翻没了是常有的事。下面是阻碍一个丈夫爱自己的妻子的理由：无论什么时候，高兴要看她就可以看见她。把你们的门关起来吧，叫你的守门人对我说："不许进来。"一被关在门外，爱情便热烈起来了！现在把钝兵器抛下来拿锋利的兵器吧。我相信就要看见那我发给你们的箭反要向我射来了。

当一个新的情郎坠入你的情网的时候，你要使他起初庆幸着能独尝欢爱，不久你便得给他一个你另有所钟，而你的恩眷并非他所独得的恐惧。假如没有这种战略，爱情便老去了。一匹骏马只有在对手超过它的时候或是要赶上它的时候才会拼命地跑。

假如我们的情焰熄了，要妒忌来使它重燃。在我呢，我承认假如别人不伤触了我，我是不会爱的。可是不要使你的情郎很明白地知道他的苦痛的原因，让他提心吊胆着，不知到底是怎么一回事。你需要假说有一个奴隶在暗地里留心你们的一举一动，和一个很厉害的男人在想法儿当场捉奸，这样是能使爱情兴奋的。

没有危险，欢乐也就没有劲儿了。即使你比泰伊斯①都自由自

---

① 雅典著名艺妓。

■ 情书写在同谋的侍女背上

在，你也得疑神疑鬼地害怕着。当你可以很容易地叫你的情郎从门里进来的时候，偏要叫他从窗口爬进来，而且你的脸儿也须装出紧张窘迫的表情。需要有一个狡猾的侍女急急忙忙地跑进来，喊着："我们糟了！"于是，你便把你的那个害怕得发抖的少年情郎随便在哪里去藏一藏。可是，在这恐惧之后，你须得叫他安安逸逸地尝一尝维纳斯的欢乐的滋味，不要叫他太吃亏。

如何去瞒过一个狡猾的男人或是一个周到的看守人等方法，我是险些忘记讲了。我希望一个妻子怕她的丈夫，我希望她是被看守得好好的，这是在礼仪上所须崇，在法律上、正义上、贞操上所须守的。可是你，刚被裁判官用小棒触着而解放了的女奴①，谁能加你以同样的监守呢？你到我的学校里来听欺骗的课程吧。

那些监视的人，即使他们有和阿耳戈斯②一样多的眼睛，只要

————————

① 这里指罗马解放奴隶时的仪式。
② 百眼巨人，是天后派去监视伊俄的。

你有决心，你一定能把他们一个个地都瞒过了。当你一个人在洗澡的时候，一个监守人如何能来妨碍你写信呢？假使你叫你的同谋的侍女把情书放在她胸脯旁边或鞋底里，监守人如何能妨碍她送出去呢？可是假如那看守人看穿了这个把戏，那么你便得叫你的同谋人露出她的背来，把情书写在她的皮肤上。阿克瑞斯①亲自很留心地管着他的女儿，可是他终究犯了错，请他做外祖父了。当在罗马有那样多的戏院子的时候，当她有时去看赛车，有时去看赛会的时候，当她去到那些她的监守人不能进去的地方②的时候，当那可怜的监守人在那大胆藏着情郎的浴池外看守着女子的衣裳的时候，一个监守人如何能管住女子呢？

当在必要时，她难道不能寻到一个口里喊着生病的女友（口说生病，倒把自己的床让给她）？那个名叫"私情女"的复制的钥匙可不是已为我们指出应该怎么样办吗？而且要到情人房里去，我们难道非从门里进去不可吗？

为要免去一个监守人的监视，我们还可以用黎阿曷士的液体③，

①阿尔戈斯国王，他的女儿达娜厄与宙斯私通，生下珀耳修斯。
②因为善良女神是不准男子们走进她的神祠去的，那些她高兴准他们进去的男子是例外。
③指酒，黎阿曷士是酒神巴克斯的别名。

■ 达娜厄 柯勒乔

就是西班牙山上出产的也可以。还有一种能叫人深深地睡去的药，它能使一个莱带河的夜压在别人的眼睛上。还有一种幸福的战略，就是叫你的同谋的侍女用欢乐的香饵迷住那个可憎的监守人，叫她用千般的温柔留住他长长久久。

可是假如只要一点小小的报效已够贿赂了那监守人，我们又何必来转许多弯，细微曲折地去想法子呢？用礼物，你们相信我啊，不论是人是神都会受诱惑的，就是宙斯大神也会上献祀物的当。所以不论是聪明人或是笨人，礼物是没有人不欢喜的。甚至是丈夫，当他收到了礼物的时候，也会装聋作哑的。可是你只要每年买给他一次就够了。他伸过一次手，自然也会时常伸手的。

我曾引为遗憾，我记起了，朋友是不可信托的。这个遗憾不仅是对男子们而发的。假如你太信任他人，别的女子就要来分尝你爱情的欢乐甜味了，而那你可以获得的兔子，也要被别人弄去了。即使是那个肯把自己的房间和床借给你的忠心的朋友，听我的话吧，她也和我有过好多次关系。不要用太漂亮的女仆，她会常常在我这儿取得她女主人的地位。

我要把自己弄成怎样啊，我这傻子，为什么袒着胸去临敌呢？为什么自己卖自己呢？鸟是不把捉自己的方法告诉捕鸟人的，鹿是不把自己逃走的路指给那要扑到它身上去的猎犬看的。我自己有什么好处呢？可是不去管他，我大方地继续着我的企图，把那可以将我处死的兵器给予利姆诺斯的女子们[①]。

你们必得要使我们自以为是被爱着（而且这是容易的事），热情是很容易坚信它所冀望着的一切的。女子只要向青年的男子瞟一瞟情眼，深深地叹息，或者问他为什么来得这样迟就够了。你们还须得加上眼泪，一种矫作的妒忌的怒，又用你们的指甲抓破了他的脸。他就立刻坚信不疑了，他便对你一往情深了。他将说："她发狂地爱着我。"尤其是那些漂亮的，常常临镜的，自以为能打动女

---

①泛指一般的女子，利姆诺斯是爱琴海中的一个岛。

幽会 弗拉戈纳尔

神的心的花花公子。可是无论如何，假如受了一次冒犯，你们切不可把不高兴表现得太露骨，知道了你的情郎另外有一个情人，你切不可气得发昏！

而且不要轻易地相信！太轻易地相信是多么的危险啊！普洛克里斯①已给了你们一个证明的例子了。

在那繁花披丽的含笑的叙美托斯山旁，有一口圣泉。一片绿荫遮住了土地，矮矮的密树造成了一个林子，杨梅树荫着碧草，迷迭香、月桂、郁翠的番石榴熏香着空气。在那面还有许多枝叶丛密的黄杨树，袅娜的西河柳、金雀花和苍松。在和风的轻息中，一切的树叶和草都微微地颤动着。刻法罗斯是爱休息的。离开了仆役和犬，这个疲倦了的青年人常常到那个地方去闲坐。他老

———————————

① 雅典王厄瑞克透斯之女。

是这样唱："无恒的凉风啊，到我胸口来平息我的火吧。"有人听到了这几句话，记住了，轻忽地去告诉他的提心吊胆的妻子。

当普洛克里斯知道了这个她以为是情敌的"凉风"的名字后，她便昏过去了，苦痛得连话也说不出来。她的脸色变得惨白，正如那被初冬的寒风所侵的、采去了葡萄的葡萄叶，或是那累累垂挂在枝头的、已经熟了的启道奈阿的果实①，或是那还没有熟透的杨桃一样的惨白。当她清醒过来的时候，她把自己胸前的轻衫撕破，又用指甲把自己的脸儿抓破——这张脸儿是当不起这种待遇的。随后突然地披散着头发，狂怒着，在路上奔跑，好像被巴克斯的松球杖所激动了一样。到了那所说的地方时，她把她的女伴留在谷中，她亲自急忙掩掩藏藏地蹑足走进树林去。

普洛克里斯，这样鬼鬼祟祟的，你的计划是什么啊？什么热焰燃起了你的迷塞的心啊？你无疑是想着那个"凉风"，那个你所不认识的"凉风"就要来了，而你又将亲眼看见奸情了。有时你懊悔前来，因为你不愿意惊散他们；有时你自祝着，你的爱情不知道如何决定，使你的心不停地跳动。你有地点、人名、告密人和那多情的男子容易和人发生恋爱的可能性来做你的盲信的辩解。在被压倒

_____

① 指木瓜。启道奈阿是一座克里特北海岸上的古城。

的草上一看见有一个生物的足迹，她的心便立刻狂跳起来了。

　　时候已到了中午，太阳已把影子缩短了，它悬在天的正中。这时那个岂莱耐山的神祇①的后裔刻法罗斯回到树林里来了，他用泉水浇着自己的晒热了的脸。普洛克里斯，你担心地躲着，而他却躺在那块常躺的草地上，嘴里说着："温柔的和风，你来啊，而你，凉风，你也来啊。"那个不幸的普洛克里斯快乐地发现那个由于一句两可之词而起的错误了，她安心了，她的脸色也恢复原状了。她站了起来；那女子想要冲到她的丈夫的怀里去，因此她便翻动了那拦在路上的树叶。

　　刻法罗斯以为是一头野兽来了，他便用一个少年人的敏捷态度拿起了他的弓，箭已经握在他的右手中了。不幸的人，你要做什么啊？这不是野兽，留住你的箭吧。箭已射中了你的妻子了。"哎哟，"她喊着，"你射穿了一颗爱你的心了。这颗老是被刻法罗斯所伤的心。我是在不该死的时候死了，可是我却没有情敌。大地啊，当你遮覆着我时，在我是格外觉得轻巧了。那个引起我的误会的'凉风'已把我的生命带去了。我死了。哦！用你的亲爱的手把我的眼皮合下吧。"他呢，吞着沉哀，将那占有他的心的人儿的垂死的娇躯枕在

---

　　①指赫耳墨斯，刻法罗斯的父亲，生在阿尔迦地亚的岂莱耐山，又在那里长大。

臂上，他的泪水洒在那个残酷的伤痕上。可是完了，那轻信的普洛克里斯的灵魂已渐渐地从她的胸口离去，而刻法罗斯，把他的嘴唇贴在她的嘴唇上，吸取了她最后的呼吸。

■ 刻法罗斯和普洛克里斯 亚历山大·迈克

我应该不弯弯曲曲地说下去。要使我的航倦了的船快快地进港了。你不耐烦地等着我领你到宴会去，而且还想我教你关于赴宴会的门径。

你应该去得很迟，而且你的姿态也不该在灯未亮之前显露出来。等待是能够增加你的身价的。除了等待之外没有别的更好的撮合人了。假如你是丑的，那喝醉了的人的眼睛看起来就美丽了，而且夜也足够掩饰住你的缺陷了。

用你的指头撮取茶点① 吃得好看也是一种艺术。不要用没有拭

---

① 那时还没有刀叉。

干净的手去抹你的脸。在赴宴以前不要在家里先吃，可是在筵席上，却不要吃得太饱，要留一点胃口。假如帕里斯看见海伦拼命地大喝大嚼，他准会说："我得到了一个多么傻的胜利啊！"

稍稍喝些酒在女子是适宜的，维纳斯的儿子和巴克斯混在一起是很和谐的。可是你也应该叫你的头担当得起那酒，不要使你的聪敏和行动被弄昏，不要使你的眼睛看花了。一个女子喝得酩酊大醉躺在地上，那是一个多么难看的怪现象啊！来一个人就可以把她取而得之的。在席上一瞌睡就要受危险，瞌睡是冒犯贞操的好机会。

我很害羞讲下去，可是那好狄俄涅①对我说："那你所害羞的正是我们的事业。"

每个女子需要认识自己，依照你的体格，你便选择各样的姿势；同样的姿态不是适合于一切的女子的。那脸儿特别漂亮的女子应当仰卧着。那些满意自己的臀部的，须得把自己的臀部显露出来。鲁西娜②可曾遗下些皱纹在你的肚子上吗？那么，你也像那帕提亚人一样，反转了背脊交欢着。米拉尼洪把阿达朗达的腿放在自己的肩上，假如你的腿很美丽，你便得照样地搁上去。矮小的女子

---

① 维纳斯之母，此处指维纳斯。
② 司生育的女神，是赫拉或狄安娜的别名。

应当取骑士的姿势，那身子很长的忒拜女子①，赫克托耳的妻子，从不跨在她的丈夫的身上，像跨在一匹马上一样。那身体颀长的女子须得跪在床上，头稍向后弯。

假如你的腿股有青春的爱娇，而你的胸膛也是完美的，那你便斜斜地躺在床上，取这种姿势的时候，不要怕羞。你须要把你的头发披散了，像跳神诸女一样，而且转着头飘散着你的头发。要尝维纳斯的欢乐有千方百态，那最简单而最不吃力的方法就是半身侧卧在右面。可是那阿波罗的三脚椅②和生牛头的阿蒙神③都不能比我的缪斯给你更靠得住的启示。

假如我的话有几句是值得相信的，你们便受我的教吧，这是一个久长的经验的结果，我的诗是不欺你们的。女子啊，我愿维纳斯的欢乐一直透进你的骨髓里，又愿你和你的情郎分受着那种享乐！情话和琐话永远不要间断，而在你们的肉搏中，有些话是应该加进

---

① 指安德洛玛刻，她生在忒拜。
② 指一种三只脚的椅子，在那上面，德尔斐的女亚启示神意。
③ 一个利比亚的神祇，在罗马为人所崇奉。

去的。即使像你这种老天吝于赋给爱情的幽欢感觉的人，你也得假装着，用温柔的谎语，说你是感觉到那种幽欢的。那种生来麻木不仁的无法体会到幽欢的快感的女子，是多么的可怜啊！可是这种矫饰切不要被发现出来，要使你的动作和你的眼睛的表情来欺骗我们！放荡、软语和喘息是会给人一种幻觉的。我讲下去有点害羞了：这个器官也有它自己的秘密的表情。

在那维纳斯的幽欢之后去向情郎要求赠物，那是用不到什么重大的恳求的。我忘记说了，在卧房里不要让光线从窗里透进来，你的身体的好多部分是不能在日光下被人看见的。

我的话已讲完，现在已是走下那天鹅驾着的车子的时候了。正如从前男子们一样，现在女子们，我的女弟子，在她们的战利品上这样写：

"奥维德是我们的老师。"

THE ART OF LOVE

By

Ovid

Translated Out of the Latin
By
J. Lewis May

BOOK I
Finding Love

If there be anyone among you who is ignorant of the art of loving, let him read this poem and, having read it and acquired the knowledge it contains, let him address himself to Love.

By art the swift ships are propelled with sail and oar, there is art in driving the fleet chariots, and Love should by art be guided. Automedon was a skilled charioteer and knew how to handle the flowing reins, Tiphys was the pilot of the good ship Argo. I have been appointed by Venus as tutor to tender Love. I shall be known as the Tiphys and Automedon of Love. Love is somewhat recalcitrant and ofttimes refuses to do my bidding, but 'tis a boy, and boys are easily moulded. Chiron brought up the boy Achilles to the music of the lyre, and by that peaceful art softened his wild nature, he, before whom his enemies were destined so oft to tremble, who many a time struck terror even into his own companions was, so 'tis said, timid and submissive in the presence of a feeble old man, obedient to his master's voice, and held out to him for chastisement those hands whereof Hector was one day destined to feel the weight. Chiron was tutor to Achilles, I am tutor to Love, both of them formidable youngsters, both of them goddess-born. But the fiery bull has to submit to the yoke, the mettled steed vainly champs at the curb that masters him. I, too, will bring Love to heel, even though his arrows pierce my breast and he brandish over my head his flaming torch. The keener his arrows, the fiercer his fires, the more they stir me to avenge my wounds.

I shall not try, O Apollo, to convey the notion that it was from thee I learned the art which I impart, no birds came and sang it in my ear. Clio and her sisters appeared not to me, grazing my herds, O Ascra, in thy vales. Experience is my guide, give ear to the adept, true are the things I sing. Mother of Love, smile on my undertaking.

Hence, ye narrow frontlets, insignia of chastity, and ye trailing robes that half conceal the feet. I sing of love where danger is not, I sing permitted pilferings, free of all offence my verses are.

You, who for the first time are taking up arms beneath the standard of Venus, find out, in the first place, the woman you are fain to love. Your next task will be to bend her to your will, your third to safeguard that your love shall endure. This is my plan, my syllabus. This is the course my chariot will pursue, such is the goal that it will endeavour to attain.

Now, that you still are fancy-free, now is the time for you to choose a woman and say to her: "You are the only woman that I care for." She's not going to be wafted down to you from heaven on the wings of the wind. You must use your own-eyes to discover the girl that suits you. The hunter knows where to spread his nets in order to snare the stag, he knows the valley where the wild boar has his lair. The bird-catcher knows where he should spread his lime, and the fisherman knows what waters most abound in fish. And thou who seekest out the object of a lasting love, learn to know the places which the fair ones most do haunt. You won't have to put to sea in order to do that, or to undertake any distant journeys. Perseus may bring home his Andromeda from sun-scorched India, and the Phrygian swain may go to Greece to bear away his bride, Rome alone will give you a choice of such lovely women, and so many of them, that you will be forced to confess that she gathers within her own bosom all the treasures that the world can show. As numerous as the ears of corn on Gargarus, grapes in Methymna, fish in the ocean, birds in the thickets, stars in the heavens, so numerous are the beautiful girls you'll find in Rome: Venus has made her seat of empire the city of her beloved Aeneas.

If your tastes incline to a young beauty, in the very flower of girlhood, a really inexperienced girl will offer herself to your gaze, if you prefer one rather more mature, there are hundreds of young women who will take your fancy: 'twill be a veritable *embarras de richesses*. But perhaps you would rather have someone still older, still more experienced. In that case you've got a yet larger number to choose from. When the sun begins to enter the sign of the Lion, you've only got to take a stroll beneath the cool shade of Pompey's portico, or near that building adorned with foreign marbles erected by a loving mother who united her offerings to those of a dutiful son. Omit not to visit that portico which, adorned with ancient pictures, is called the portico of Livia, after its foundress. There you will see the Danaides plotting the death of their unhappy kinswomen, and their fell sire grasping in his hand a naked sword. And do not miss the festival of Adonis, mourned of Venus, and the rites celebrated every seventh day by the Syrian Jews.

Shun not the Temple of the Cow of Memphis, who persuades so many women to play the part she played to Jupiter. Even the Forum, strange though it sound, is propitious to love-making. Lawyers are by no means proof against the fiery shafts of Love. Hard by the marble temple sacred to Venus, where plays the waters of the Appian fount, many an advocate has fallen a victim to the snares of Love, for the man who defends his client cannot always defend himself. In such a pass, words sometimes fail even the most learned orator. The tables are turned and he finds himself obliged to plead his own cause. From her temple close at hand, Venus laughs to see him in such a quandary. A patron but a little while ago, he would now rejoice to be a client.

But it is especially at the theatre you should lay your snares, that is where you may hope to have your desires fulfilled. Here you will find women to your taste: one for a moment's dalliance, another to fondle and caress, another to have all for your own. Even as the ants that come and go in long battalions with their stores of food, or as the bees, when they have found plants to plunder of their honey, hover hither and thither among the thyme and the flowers, so, and no less numerous, you may see crowds of lovely women, gaily dressed, hastening away to the theatre. I have often found it difficult to choose from such a galaxy. They come to see and more important still, to be seen! The theatre's the place where modesty acts a fall.

It was you, Romulus, who first mingled the cares of love with public games, that far-off day when the rape of the Sabine women gave wives to your warriors who had waited for them so long. No curtains then hung in the marble theatre, nor was the stage made red with liquid saffron. In those days branches from the woods of the Palatine were the only adornment of our simple stage. The people sat on seats of turf, their heads canopied with boughs.

As soon as he had sat him down, each Roman looked about, marking the woman whom he most desired, giving free play to the thoughts that surged within him. Whilst to the sound of a rustic pipe an actor strikes his foot three times upon the levelled earth, amid the unforced applause of the expectant throng (for in those days applause was neither bought nor sold), Romulus signed to his men to seize upon their prey. In a trice, with shouts that made their object clear, they laid their eager hands upon the cowering women. Even as the weak and timid doves flee before an eagle, even as a young lamb quails at the sight of a wolf, so shuddered the Sabine women when they beheld these fierce warriors making towards them. Every one turned pale, terror spread throughout the throng, but it showed itself in different ways. Some tore their hair, some swooned away, some wept in silence, some called vainly for their mothers, some sobbed aloud, others seemed stupefied with fear, some stood transfixed, and others tried to flee. Nevertheless, the Romans carry off the women, sweet booty for their beds, and to many of them, terror lends an added charm.

If one shows herself too rebellious and refuses to follow her ravisher, he picks her up and, pressing her lovingly to his bosom, exclaims: "Why with tears do you thus dim the lovely radiance of your eyes? What your father is to your mother, that will I be to you." O Romulus, you are the only one who has ever known how to reward his soldiers, for such pay, I would willingly enrol myself beneath your banners. Ever since those days, the theatres, faithful to this ancient custom, have always been a dangerous lure to loveliness.

Forget not the arena where mettled steeds strive for the palm of Victory. This circus, where an immense concourse of people is gathered, is very favourable to Love. There, if you would express the secret promptings of your heart, there is no need for you to talk upon your fingers, or to watch for signs to tell you what is in your fair one's mind. Sit close beside her, as close as you are able, there's nothing to prevent. The narrowness of the space compels you to press against her and, fortunately for you, compels her to acquiesce. Then, of course, you must think of some means of starting the conversation. Begin by saying the sort of thing people generally do say on such occasions. Some horses are seen entering the stadium, ask her the name of their owner, and whoever she favours, you should follow suit. And when the solemn procession of the country's gods and goddesses passes along, be sure and give a rousing cheer for Venus, your protectress. If as not infrequently befalls, a speck of dust lights on your fair one's breast, flick it off with an airy finger, and if there's nothing there, flick it off just the same, anything is good enough to serve as a pretext for paying her attention. Is her dress dragging on the ground? Gather it up, and take special care that nothing soils it. Perchance, to reward you for your kindness, she'll grant you the favour of letting you see her leg. And then again, you must keep an eye on the people seated in the row behind and see that no one thrusts his knee into her soft shoulders. The merest trifle is enough to win these butterfly ladies. Why, hosts of men have succeeded with a woman merely by the attentive manner in which they have arranged a cushion for her, or fanned her with a fan, or put a stool beneath her dainty feet. Both the circus and the forum afford opportunities for a love-affair. Love often delights to try his strength there, and many a man, who came to see another wounded, finds that he has been pinked himself. While he is talking and stroking her hand, asking for the race-card and, having put his money on, is inquiring what has won, an arrow pierces him before he knows where he is, he heaves a sigh and, instead of being a mere spectator of the combat, he finds himself a victim.

Did we not see this happen quite recently, when Caesar offered us the spectacle of a sea-fight showing the Persian and the Athenian ships in action. Then indeed, from both seas, youths and maidens flocked to see the show and the whole world was gathered within the City. Which of us, in that vast throng, found not a woman worthy of his love, and, alas, how many were tortured by a foreign flame.

But lo, Caesar makes ready to complete the conquest of the world! Ye far-off countries of the East, to our laws shall ye submit, and you, ye arrogant Parthians, shall be punished as ye deserve. Rejoice, shades of Crassus, and you, ye Roman Eagles, ashamed at your long sojourn in barbarian hands, be of good cheer, your avenger is at hand. Scarce has he essayed to wield his arms, and yet he proves himself a skilful leader. Though he himself is but a boy, he wages a war unsuited to his boyish years. O, ye of little faith, vex not your souls about the age of the gods! Courage in a Caesar does not wait upon the years. Genius divine outpaces time and brooks not the tedium of tardy growth. Hercules was still no more than a child when he crushed the serpents in his baby hands. Even in the cradle he proved himself a worthy son of Jove. And you, Bacchus, still glowing with youthful radiance, how mighty wast thou when India trembled at thy conquering Thyrsi! With the auspices and with the courage of thy sire shalt thou wield thine arms, young Caesar, with the courage and with the auspices of thy sire shalt thou overthrow thine enemies. Such a beginning becomes the name thou bearest. Today thou art Prince of the Youths, one day thou shalt be Prince of the Elders. Since thou hast brothers, avenge thy slaughtered brethren, and since thou hast a sire, defend thy father's rights. It is thy father, thy country's father, who hath armed thee, what time the foe is violently wrestling the sceptre from a parent's struggling hand. Thy sacred cause shall triumph o'er the perjured foe, justice and piety shall march beneath thy standards. The righteousness of our cause shall overcome the Parthians, arms shall drive the victory home, and so to Latium's riches, the wealth of the Orient shall my young hero add. Mars, his sire, and thou Caesar, his sire too, a god the one, the other soon a god to be, watch over him and keep him from all harm. I can read the hidden secrets of the future. Aye, thou wilt conquer. I will sing thy glory in verses consecrate to thee, with a loud voice I will sound thy praise. Standing erect will I depict thee, and urging thy warriors to the combat. Grant that my song be not unworthy of the prowess that it celebrates! I will sing of the Parthian turning to flee, and of the Roman facing the arrows aimed at him by the flying foe. What, Parthian, dost thou leave to the conquered, who seekest victory in flight? Henceforth, for thee Mars forebodeth nought but ill.

That day shall dawn, O fairest of mankind, when, resplendent with gold, by four white horses drawn, thou shalt pass within the City walls. Before thee, laden with chains, shall walk the conquered leaders, nor shall they then, as erst they did, seek safety in flight.

Young men and maidens shall with joy behold the sight, and with gladness shall all hearts be filled. Then if some fair one shall ask of thee the name of this or that defeated monarch, what all these emblems mean, what country this, what mountain that, or what that river yonder represents, answer at once, anticipate her questions, speak up with confidence, and even when your mind's a blank, speak up as if you had the knowledge pat. "Here's the Euphrates, with his sedgy crown, and that old fellow there, with sky-blue hair, why, he's the Tigris, and those? Hum! Well, they're Armenians. That woman yonder? She is Persia, where the son of Danaë was born. That town till lately rose up amid the vales of Achaemenes. That prisoner there, or that other one yonder? Oh, they are captured generals." And if you know them, give their names. If you don't, invent them.

Dinners and banquets offer easy access to women's favour, and the pleasures of the grape are not the only entertainment you may find there. Love, with rosy cheeks, often presses in her frail hands the amphora of Bacchus. As soon as his wings are drenched with wine, Cupid grows drowsy and stirs not from his place. But anon he'll be up and shaking the moisture from his wings, and woe betide the man or woman who receives a sprinkling of this burning dew. Wine fills the heart with thoughts of love and makes it prompt to catch on fire. All troubles vanish, put to flight by copious draughts.

Then is the time for laughter, the poor man plucks up courage and imagines he's a millionaire. To the deuce with worries and troubles! Brows unpucker and hearts expand, every tongue's inspired by frankness, and calls a spade a spade. We've often lost our heart to a pretty girl at dinner. Bringing love and wine together is adding fuel to fire indeed. Don't judge a woman by candle-light, it's deceptive. If you really want to know what she's like, look at her by daylight, and when you're sober. It was broad daylight, and under the open sky, that Paris looked upon the three goddesses and said to Venus: "You are lovelier than your two rivals." Night covers a multitude of blemishes and imperfections. At night there is no such thing as an ugly woman! If you want to look at precious stones, or coloured cloth, you take them out into the light of day, and it's by daylight you should judge a woman's face and figure.

But if I'm to mention all the places favourable to woman-hunting, I might as well attempt to number the sands of the seashore. Of course, there's Baiae, with white sails gleaming out in the bay, and its hot sulphur spring. Many a bather, who has gone there for his health, comes away and saying: "Those precious baths are not such healthy things as people make out." Not far from the gates of Rome, behold the temple of Diana shaded by trees, the scene of many a hard-fought contest for the prize of Love. Because she's a virgin and hates the darts of Love, Diana has inflicted many a wound there, and will inflict many more.

Thus far my Muse, borne in her chariot with wheels of different height, has, told you, would-be lover, where to seek your prey, and how to lay your snares. Now I'll teach you how to captivate and hold the woman of your choice. This is the most important part of all my lessons. Lovers of every land, lend an attentive ear to my discourse, let goodwill warm your hearts, for I am going to fulfil the promises I made you.

First of all, be quite sure that there isn't a woman who cannot be won, and make up your mind that you will win her. Only you must prepare the ground. Sooner would the birds cease their song in the springtime, or the grasshopper be silent in the summer, or the hares turn and give chase to a hound of Maenalus, than a woman resist the tender wooing of a youthful lover. Perhaps you think she doesn't want to yield. You're wrong. She wants to in her heart of hearts. Stolen love is just as sweet to women as it is to us. Man is a poor dissembler, woman is much more skilful in concealing her desire. If all the men agreed that they would never more make the first advance, the women would soon be fawning at our feet. Out in the springy meadow the heifer lows with longing for the bull, the mare neighs at the approach of the stallion. With men and women love is more restrained, and passion is less fierce. They keep within bounds. Need I mention Byblis, who burned for her brother with an incestuous flame, and hanged herself to expiate her crime? Or Myrrha, who loved her father, but not as a father should be loved, and now her shame is hidden by the bark of the tree that covered her. O sweetly scented tree, the tears which she distils, to us give perfume and recall the ill-fated maid's unhappy name.

One day in wood-crowned Ida's shady vale, a white bull went wandering by. The pride of all the herd was he. Between his horns was just a single spot of black, save for that mark, his body was as white as milk, and all the heifers of Gnossus and of Cydonia sighed for the joy of his caress. Pasiphaë conceived a passion for him and viewed with jealous eye the loveliest among the heifers. There's no gain saying it, Crete with her hundred cities, Crete, liar though she be, cannot deny it. 'Tis said that Pasiphaë, with hands unused to undertake such toil, tore from the trees their tenderest shoots, culled from the meadows bunches of sweet grass and hastened to offer them to her beloved bull. Whithersoever he went, she followed him, nothing would stay her. She recked not of her spouse, the bull had conquered Minos. "What avails it, Pasiphaë, to deck yourself in costly raiment? How can your lover of such riches judge?" Wherefore, mirror in hand, dost thou follow the wandering herd up to the mountain top? Wherefore dost thou for ever range thy hair? Look in thy mirror: " 'twill tell thee thou art no meet mistress for a bull. Ah, what wouldst thou not have given if Nature had but armed thy brow with horns! If Minos still doth hold a corner in thy heart, cease this adulterous love, or if thou must deceive thy spouse, at least deceive him with a man." She hearkens not, but, fleeing from his royal couch, she ranges ever on and on, through forest after forest, like to a Bacchante full of the spirit that unceasingly torments her. How often, looking with jealous anger on a heifer, did she exclaim: "How then can she find favour in his sight? See how she prances before him on the green. Fool, she doubtless deems that thus she is lovelier in his eyes." Then, at her command, the hapless beast is taken from the herd and sent to bow her head beneath the yoke, or else, pretending to offer sacrifice to the gods, she orders her to be slain, at the altar, and then with joy fingers o'er the entrails of her rival. How often, under the guise of one who offers sacrifice, hath she appeased the alleged displeasure of the gods, and waving the bleeding trophies in her hand exclaimed: "Go, get thee to my lover, please go him now!" Now she would be Europa, now she would be Io, the one because she was a heifer, the other because a bull bore her on his back. Howbeit, deceived by the image of a cow of maple wood, the king of the herd performed with her the act of love, and by the offspring was the sire betrayed.

Had that other Cretan girl been able to forego her passion for Thyestes (but how hard it is for a woman to love one man alone), Poebus would not have been compelled to stay his steeds in mid-career, and to have driven his chariot back again towards the Dawn. The daughter of Nisus, because she had stolen from the father's head the fatal lock of hair, is evermore beset by ravening dogs. The son of Atreus, though he escaped the perils of the battlefield and the ocean, died beneath the dagger of his cruel spouse. Who has listened to the love story of Creusa? Who has not hated the mad fury of Medea, a mother stained with her children's blood? Phoenix, the son of Amyntor, wept with his sightless orbs. You, ye steeds, in your terror, tore Hippolytus in pieces. Wherefore, Phineus, didst thou put out the eyes of thy innocent sons? Upon thine own head will that punishment return. Such are the consequences of woman's unbridled passion. Fiercer it is than ours, with more of frenzy in it.

Be, then, of good cheer, and never doubt that you will conquer. Not one woman in a thousand will seriously resist. Whether a pretty woman grants or withholds her favours, she always likes to be asked for them. Even if you are repulsed, you don't run any danger. But why should a woman refuse? People don't resist the temptation of new delights. We always deem that other people are more fortunate than ourselves. The crop is always better in our neighbour's field, his cows more rich in milk.

Now the first thing you have to do is to get on good terms with the fair one's maid. She can make things easy for you. Find out whether she is fully in her mistress's confidence, and if she knows all about her secret dissipations. Leave no stone unturned to win her over. Once you have her on your side, the rest is easy. Let her watch for a favourable time (that's a precaution that doctors do not neglect), let her take advantage of the moment when her mistress may more easily be persuaded, when she is more likely to surrender to a lover's solicitations. At such times, the whole world seems *couleur de rose* to her, gaiety dances in her eyes as the golden wheat-ears dance in a fertile field. When the heart is glad, when it is not gripped by sorrow, it opens and expands. Then it is that Love slips gently into its inmost folds. So long as Ilion was plunged in mourning, her warriors kept the Greeks at bay, it was when she was rejoicing and making merry that she received within her walls the fatal horse with its armed freight. Choose, too, the moment when your charmer is smarting from the insult of a rival, make her see in you a means of wiping off the score. When, in the morning, she is doing her mistress's hair, let the maid foment her anger, let her press on with sail and oar and, sighing, murmur, "Why not, Madam, pay him out in his own coin?" Then let her talk of you, let her adroitly sing your praises and swear that you poor fellow are wildly in love with her. But don't lose any time, for fear the wind should drop and the sails hang limp. Fragile as ice, a woman's anger is a transient thing.

"What about the maid herself?" you ask, "Is it well to win her favours first?" Now that's a ticklish business. Sometimes it stimulates their zeal, sometimes the opposite's the case. One girl will do her utmost for her mistress, another will want to keep you for herself. The only thing is just to try, and see how it turns out. On the whole, my advice to you is "Don't". I shouldn't risk these steep and dangerous by-ways myself. If you keep with me, you'll be on the right road. If, however, you are taken with the servant's charms, if you find her as pretty as she's zealous, win the mistress first, and afterwards turn your attention to the maid, but don't begin with her. Only I warn you, if you have any faith in my teaching, if my words are not dispersed by the winds over the seas, don't make the attempt at all unless you carry it right through. Once she is well involved, she won't give you away. The bird, with its wings well limed, won't fly far, the boar can't escape from the nets, once a fish is on the hook, he can't get away. So my advice to you is, push your attack well home, and don't be in a hurry to withdraw your forces when the victory's won. Thus she'll be your companion in crime, and she'll never betray you, she'll tell you everything you want to know about her mistress. The great thing is to be careful. If you keep your goings-on with the maid quite dark, you'll hear about everything her mistress does.

Some people think that time and the seasons only concern farmers and seafaring men. They're wrong. Just as there's a time to sow, and a time to sail, so there's a time to begin on a pretty girl. Success often depends on your seizing the right moment to open the attack. Keep clear of her birthday, for example, and shun the Kalends of March. Don't begin when there's a big show on at the circus. That would prove the winter of your discontent, when the stormy winds would blow, and you'd do well to hold off. If you launch the ship then, you'll be lucky if you're washed ashore clinging to a spar. If you want a really good opportunity, wait for the anniversary of the fatal day when Roman blood incarnadined the waters of the Allia, or for that one day out of the seven on which the Syrian Jew will do no manner of work. Above all, don't go near her on her birthday, or indeed on any day when you're expected to give a present. However much you try to wriggle out of it, she'll make you buy her something. A woman always knows how to exploit an ardent lover. Some pedlar fellow will be sure to turn up, and since buying's a mania with them all, she'll be sure to find the very things she wants. She'll ask you to look at 'em, then she'll kiss you, and say, "Oh, do buy me that. It'll last for years, it's just the very thing I want, and you couldn't buy me anything I should like more." It's no good saying you haven't got the money on you, she'll ask you to draw a cheque, and then you'll curse the day you learned to write. And how many times you'll have to give her something for her birthday! Every time she wants anything very special, she'll have a birthday. And then she'll come grieving some pretended loss, she'll come to you with eyes all red with weeping and tell you she's lost one of her precious ear-rings. That's the little game they play. Then they'll keep on asking you to lend them money, and once they've got it, I wouldn't give much for your chances of getting it back. You can look on that as gone, and they won't give you so much as a "thank you". Why, if I'd got ten mouths and ten tongues, I couldn't tell you all the tricks our ladies of the demi-monde get up to.

In the first place, it's best to send her a letter, just to pave the way. In it you should tell her how you dote on her, pay her pretty compliments and say all the nice things lovers always say. Achilles gave way to Priam's supplications. Even the gods are moved by the voice of entreaty. And promise, promise, promise. Promises will cost you nothing. Everyone's a millionaire where promises are concerned. Hope, if only she is duly fostered, holds out a long time. She's a deceitful goddess, but a very useful one. If you give your mistress something, she may give you your conge. She will have had her *quid pro quo*. Always make her think you're just about to give, but never really do so. Thus your farmer will keep on manuring a barren field, hoping it will produce a crop some day. Your gambler will keep throwing good money after bad, in hopes of redeeming all his losses, and thus his greed falls a victim to his hope of gain. The really great problem, the problem that takes all a man's skill to solve, is to win a woman's favours without making her a present. If you succeed in that, she will go on giving, so as not to lose the guerdon of the favours she has already bestowed. So send off your letter and couch it in the sweetest terms, it should be a sort of preliminary reconnaissance and pave the way to her heart. A few characters written on an apple led the young Cydippe astray and, when she had read them, the rash girl found she was ensnared by her own words.

Take my advice, my youthful fellow-citizens, and study the fine arts, not only that you may champion the cause of some trembling dependent. The common herd, the austere judge, and those superior people, the senators, are not the only people who are moved by eloquence. But don't show your hand, and don't be in too much of a hurry to display your powers of speech. And don't put on the professorial style. Who but an idiot would write to his mistress as though he were addressing a meeting. A show-off letter will often turn a woman against you. Be quite natural, quite simple, but engaging. In a word, say just what you would say if you were speaking to her. If she refuses your letter and sends it back unread, don't give up, hope for the best and try again. The unruly bull bows to the yoke in time, and, in time, the most obstreperous colt gets broken in. You can wear through an iron ring by continuous friction, the ploughshare wears away every day against the soil it cleaves. What could you have harder than a rock, or less hard than water? Nevertheless, water will wear away the hardest rock. So keep pegging away, and, given time, you'll get your way with Penelope herself. Troy held out a long time, but it fell at last. Suppose she reads your letter but doesn't answer. So be it. Only keep her busy reading. Since she has condescended to read, she'll answer some fine day. Everything comes gradually and at its appointed hour. Peradventure she'll write in a huff and tell you to cease annoying her. If she does, she's trembling lest you take her at her word. She wants you to go on, although she tells you not to. So go on, and soon you'll have your heart's desire.

If you see your mistress being borne along on her litter, go up to her as if by accident, and say what you've got to say in vague ambiguous language, for fear some busybody should be listening. If you see her hanging about under some portico, as if she didn't know what to do with herself, go and walk there too. Sometimes get in front of her, and sometimes drop behind. Don't be bashful about getting clear of the crowd and crossing over to her side. Don't, on any account, let her go to the theatre, looking her loveliest, without your being there to see. Her bare shoulders will give you something charming to contemplate. And you can look at her and admire her at your leisure, and speak to her with eyes and gestures. Applaud the actor that plays the girl's part, applaud still more the man that plays the lover. If she stands up, stand up too, and while she is sitting, keep your seat, don't worry about the time, squander it as your mistress may require.

And don't, for heaven's sake, have your hair waved, or use powder on your skin. Leave such foppishness as that to the effeminate priests who wail their Phrygian chants in honour of Cybele. Simplicity in dress is what best befits a man. Theseus conquered Ariadne without troubling about the way his hair was done. Phaedra fell in love with Hippolytus, who certainly was not a dandy. Adonis, a simple woodlander, was the idol of a goddess. Study to be clean, let your skin be tanned in the open air, wear well-cut clothes, and see there are no spots on them. Have a clean tongue, and let your teeth be free from tartar, and don't slop about in boots that are two or three sizes too big for you.

Don't let your hair stick up in tufts on your head, see that your hair and your beard are decently trimmed. See also that your nails are clean and nicely filed, don't have any hair growing out of your nostrils, take care that your breath is sweet, and don't go about reeking like a billy-goat. All other toilet refinements leave to the women or to perverts.

But lo, Bacchus is summoning his bard, propitious to lovers, he fosters the fires with which he is consumed himself. Ariadne was wandering distraught along the lonely wave-beaten shores of Naxos. Scarce had sleep departed from her eyes, and she wore but an airy shift, her feet were bare and her fair tresses were blowing about her shoulders. To the heedless billows she was crying wildly for her Theseus, and tears flowed in torrents down her cheeks. She cried aloud and wept at the same time. But both enhanced her beauty. "Oh, the faithless one," she cried, beating her tender bosom again and again, "he has abandoned me. Oh, what will become of me! What will be my fate!" She spake. And on a sudden, drums and cymbals beaten and tossed by frenzied hands resounded along the shore. Stricken with terror, she fell gasping out a few broken words, and the blood faded from her lifeless corpse. But lo, the Maenads, with their hair floating wildly out behind them, and the light-footed Satyrs, the rout that leads the procession of Apollo, came upon the scene. Behold, old Silenus, reeling-ripe as usual, who can scarce keep his seat on the ass that staggers beneath the heavy burden. He pursues the Maenads, who flee from him and mock him as they flee, and as he belabours his long-eared beast with his staff, the unskilful cavalier tumbles head-foremost from his steed. And all the Satyrs shout: "Up with you, old man Silenus, up with you again!"

Meanwhile from his lofty chariot with vine branches all bedecked, the god, handling the golden reins, drives on his team of tigers. The girl, in losing Theseus, had lost her colour and her voice. Thrice she attempted flight, thrice did fear paralyse her steps, she shuddered, she trembled like the tapering stem or the slender reed that sways at the slightest breath. "Banish all thy fears," cried the god, "In me thou findest a tenderer, more faithful lover than Theseus. Daughter of Minos, thou shalt be the bride of Bacchus. Thy guerdon shall be a dwelling in the sky, thou shalt be a new star and thy bright diadem shall be a guide to the pilot uncertain of his course." So saying he leapt from his chariot lest his tigers should affright her. The sand yielded beneath his feet. Clasping to his breast the swooning, unresisting girl, he bore her away. For a god may do as he wills, and who shall say him nay. Then some sang *Hymenaee*, and some sang *Evion Evoë*! And to these strains the god and his bride consummated their spousals on the sacred couch.

When, then, you find yourself at a feast where the wine is flowing freely, and where a woman shares the same couch with you, pray to that god whose mysteries are celebrated during the night, that the wine may not overcloud thy brain. 'Tis then thou mayest easily hold converse with thy mistress in hidden words whereof she will easily divine the meaning. A drop of wine will enable you to draw sweet emblems on the table wherein she will read the proof of the love you have for her. Fix well thine eyes on her and so confirm the message of thy love. Ofttimes, without a word being spoken, the eyes can tell a wondrous tale. When she has drunk, be thou the first to seize the cup, and where her lips have touched, there press thine own and drink. Choose thou the dainties that her fingers have lightly touched, and as thou reachest for them, let thy hand softly encounter hers.

Be courteous to her husband too. Nothing could better serve

your plans than to be in his good graces. If, when the dice are thrown, chance crowns thee king of the feast, yield him the honour, take off thy wreath and place it on his brow. Whether he be thy equal or inferior matters not. Let him be served the first, and flatter him in everything you say. The surest and most common means to success is to deceive him under the cloak of friendship. But though 'tis sure and common, 'tis none the less a crime. Sometimes in love the ambassador goes too far and doth exceed the terms of his mandate.

Now I will lay down the limits thou shouldst observe in drinking: never drink enough to cloud your brain or make your gait unsteady, avoid the quarrels that are born of wine and be not prompt to take offence. Follow not the example of Eurytion, who, like a fool, gave up the ghost because he had drunk too much. The food and the wine should inspire a gentle gaiety. If you have a voice, sing, and if your limbs are supple, dance, in short, do everything you can to make a good impression. Downright drunkenness is a loathsome thing, simulated inebriety may serve a useful purpose. Let your tongue falter with a cunning stammer, pretend it's difficult for you to pronounce your words, so that whatever you do or say a little on the risky side may be put down to the fact that you've had too much liquor. Drink to your mistress, and do it openly, and drink to the man that shares her bed—and, under your breath, curse her lawful spouse. When the guests rise up to go, you'll have a good chance to get very close to your lady. Mingle in the crowd, contrive to get near her, press her side with your fingers and rub your foot against hers.

And now, we'll say, you've got her to yourself. Now you can talk to her. Avaunt then, rustic modesty! Fortune and Venus favour the brave. Don't ask me to tell you what to say, just take and begin, the words will come fast enough without you having to search for them. You must play the lover for all you're worth. Tell her how you are pining for her, do everything you know to win her over. She will believe you fast enough. Every woman thinks herself attractive, even the plainest is satisfied with the charms she deems that she possesses. And, then, how often it has happened that the man who begins by feigning love ends by falling in love in real earnest. Ali, my fair ones, look with indulgent eye on those that give themselves a lover's airs, the love, now feigned, will soon be love indeed.

By subtle flatteries you may be able to steal into her heart, even as the river insensibly o'erflows the banks which fringe it. Never cease to sing the praises of her face, her hair, her taper fingers and her dainty foot. The coldest beauty is moved by praises of her charms, and even the innocent and greenest girl takes pride and pleasure in the care of her good looks. If it were not so, wherefore should Juno and Minerva blush even now to have failed to carry off the prize for loveliness, in the woods of Ida? See that peacock there, if you belaud his plumage, he'll spread his tail with pride, but if in silence you look at him, he'll never show his treasures. The courser, in the chariot race, is proud of the admiration bestowed on his well-groomed mane and his proudly arched neck. Be not backward in your promises, women are drawn on by promises, and swear by all the gods that you'll be as good as your word. Jove, from his high abode, looks down and laughs on lovers' perfidies, and gives them to Aeolus for the winds to sport with. Often he swore to Juno by the Styx that he'd be faithful, and he broke his vows. His example should lend us courage.

'Tis well that the gods should exist and well that we should believe in them. Let us bring offerings of wine and frankincense to their immemorial altars. They are not sunk in indolent repose and slothful ease. Live then in innocence, for the gods are omnipresent. Fulfil the trust that has been reposed in you, observe the precepts of religion, have nought to do with fraud, stain not your hands with blood. If you are wise, practise deceit on women alone, for that you may do with impunity, but in all other matters let your word be your bond. Deceive them that are deceivers, women for the most part are a perfidious race, let them fall into the snares which they themselves have prepared. Egypt, so they tell, being deprived of the rains which fertilise its soil, had suffered nine years of continuous drought when Thrasius came to Busiris and announced that Jove could be propitiated by the shedding of a stranger's blood. "Then," said Busiris, "thou shalt be the first victim offered to the god, thou shalt be that stranger-guest to whom Egypt shall owe the rain from heaven." Phalaris, too, caused the ferocious Perillus to be burnt within the brazen bull which he had fashioned, and the ill-fated craftsman was the first to put his handiwork to the proof. Both penalties were just, and indeed there is no law more righteous than that the contrivers of death should perish by their own inventions. Wherefore, since a lie should pay for a lie, let woman be deceived and let her blame no one but herself for the treachery whereof she set the example.

Tears, too, are a mighty useful resource in the matter of love. They would melt a diamond. Make a point, therefore, of letting your mistress see your face all wet with tears. Howbeit, if you cannot manage to squeeze out any tears—and they won't always flow just when you want them to—put your finger in your eyes. What lover of experience does not know how greatly kisses add cogency to tender speeches? If she refuses to be kissed, kiss her all the same. She may struggle to begin with. "Horrid man!" she'll say, but if she fights, 'twill be a losing battle. Nevertheless, don't be too rough with her and hurt her dainty mouth. Don't give her cause to say that you're a brute. And if, after you've kissed her, you fail to take the rest, you don't deserve even what you've won. What more did you want to come to the fulfilment of your desires? Oh, shame on you! It was not your modesty, it was your stupid clownishness. You would have hurt her in the struggle, you say? But women like being hurt. What they like to give, they love to be robbed of. Every woman taken by force in a hurricane of passion is transported with delight, nothing you could give her pleases her like that. But when she comes forth scatheless from a combat in which she might have been taken by assault, however pleased she may try to look, she is sorry in her heart. Phoebe was raped, and so, too, was her sister Hilaria, and yet they loved their ravishers not a whit the less.

A well-known story, but one that may well be told again, is that of Achilles and the maid of Scyros. Venus had rewarded Paris for the homage he had paid to her beauty when at the foot of Mount Ida she triumphed over her two rivals. From a far-off country a new daughter-in-law has come to Priam, and within the walls of Ilion there dwells an Argive bride. The Greeks swore to avenge the outraged husband, for an affront to one was an affront to all. Howbeit, Achilles (shame on him if he had not yielded to a mother's prayers) had disguised his manhood beneath the garments of a girl. "What dost thou there, descendant of Aeacus? Dost thou busy thyself with carding wool? Is that a task for a man? It is by other arts of Pallas that thou shouldst seek for fame. What hast thou to do with work-baskets? Thine arm is made to bear the shield. How comes this distaff in the hand that should lay Hector low? Cast from thee these spindles, and let thy doughty hand brandish a spear from Pelion." Once chance brought Achilles and the royal maiden together in the same bedchamber, and then the onslaught she underwent swiftly revealed to her the sex of her companion. Doubtless she yielded only to superior force, so we must of course believe, but at least she was not angry that force gained the day. "Stay yet awhile," she said entreatingly, when Achilles, eager to be gone, had laid aside the distaff to seize his valiant arms. What then has become of this alleged violence? Wherefore, Deidamia, wilt thou retain with pleading tones the author of thy downfall?

True, if modesty does not permit a woman to make the first advance, it nevertheless delights her to yield when her lover takes the initiative. In truth a lover reposes too much confidence in his good looks if he thinks that a woman will be the first to ask. 'Tis for him to begin, for him to entreat her, and to his supplications she will incline her ear. Ask and thou shalt receive, she only waits to be implored. Tell her the cause and origin of your desire. Jove bent the knee to the heroines of old times, and for all his greatness, none ever came of her own accord to entreat him. If, however, you only get disdain for all your pains, draw back and press your suit no farther. Many women long for what eludes them, and like not what is offered them. Cool off, don't let her think you too importunate. Do not betray the hope of too swift a victory, let Love steal in disguised as Friendship. I've often seen a woman thus disarmed, and friendship ripen into love.

A pale complexion ill becomes a sailor. The rays of the sun and the salt spray should have tanned his features, nor does it suit the husbandman who, with plough or heavy rakes, is for ever turning up the soil in the open air, and ye who strive for the athlete's crown of olive, it would ill beseem you to have too white a skin. But every lover should be pale, pallor is the symptom of Love, it is the hue appropriate to Love. So, deceived by your paleness, let your mistress be tenderly solicitous for your health. Orion was pale with love when he wandered after Lyrice in the woods of Dirce. Pale, too, was Daphnis for the Naiad that disdained him. Thinness, too, is an index to the feelings, and be not ashamed to veil your shining hair beneath the hood. Sleepless nights make thin a young man's body. So that thou mayest come to the fruition of your desires, shrink not from exciting pity, that all who behold you may exclaim, "Why, poor wretch, you are in love!" Shall I complain aloud or only whisper it, how virtue is on every side confounded with vice? Friendship and constancy are both but empty names. You cannot with safety tell your friend all the charms of the woman you adore, if he believed what you said of her, he would straightway become your rival. But, you will argue, the grandson of Actor stained not the couch of Achilles, Phaedra erred not, at least, not in favour of Pirithoüs, Pylades loved Hermione with a love as chaste as that which Phoebus bore for Pallas, or as the love of Castor and Pollux for their sister Helen. But if you count on miracles like that, you might as well expect to cull apples from the tamarisk, or to gather honey in the middle of a river. Vice is so inviting, and each man seeks but to gratify his own pleasure. And pleasure is sweetest when 'tis paid for by another's pain. Shun those men you think you can rely on, and you'll be safe. Beware alike of kinsman, brother, and dear friend. They are the people who generally make the trouble.

I was on the point of ending here, but let me add that women are things of many moods. You must adapt your treatment to the special case. The same soil is not equally good for everything. This land is good for the vine, and this for olives, and here's the place for corn. You'll find as many dispositions in the world as you meet with different figures and faces. A clever man will know how to adapt himself to this diversity of temper and disposition, and suit his conversation to the needs of the hour, even as Proteus, who is now a graceful wave, now a lion, now a tree, and now a boar with bristling hide. It's the same with fish, some you spear, others you take with the line, and others again in the encircling net. Different methods suit different people. You must vary them according to the age of your mistresses. An old hind will descry your machinations from afar. If you display too much skill to the novice, and too much enterprise to the bashful, you'll frighten her and put her on her guard. Thus it sometimes happens that a woman, who has feared to yield to the caresses of a man of breeding, will fall into the arms of a worthless knave.

A part of my enterprise is now achieved, though more remains behind. Here then let us heave the anchor and give ourselves a little rest.

BOOK II
On Making Love Last

Sing, and sing again Io Paean! The quarry that I was hot upon hath fallen into my toils. Let the joyous lover set the laurel crown upon my brow and raise me to a loftier pinnacle than Hesiod of Ascra or the blind old bard of Maceonia. Thus did Priam's son, crowding on all sail in his flight from warlike Amyclae, bear with him his ravished bride, and thus, too, Hippodamia, did Pelops, in his victorious chariot, carry thee far from thy native land.

Young man, why wilt thou haste so fast? Thy vessel sails the open sea, and the harbour to which I am steering thee is still far off. It sufficeth not that my verses have brought thy mistress to thine arms, my art hath taught thee how to win her, it must also teach thee how to keep her. Though it be glorious to make conquests, it is still more glorious to retain them. The former is sometimes the work of chance, the latter is always the work of skill.

Queen of Cythera, and thou her son, if ever ye looked with kindly eye upon me, 'tis, above all, today that of your succour I have need. And thee too, Erato, I invoke, for 'tis, from love thou dost derive thy name. Great is the enterprise I have in mind. I am going to tell how Love, that fickle child, may captured be, Love that is wandering up and down in this wide world of ours. Airy is he, possessed of wings to fly withal. How shall we stay his flight?

Minos had left no stone unturned to prevent the escape of his stranger-guest. Yet he dared, with wings, to cleave himself a way. When Daedalus had imprisoned the monster half-man, half-bull, that his erring mother had conceived, he spoke to Minos and saying: "O thou who art so just, set a term to my exile, let my native land receive my ashes. If the Fates forbid that I should live in my own country, grant at least that I may die there. Grant that my son may return to his home, even if his father beseeches thee in vain. Or if thou hast no pity for the child, let thy compassion light upon the father." Thus spake Daedalus, but in vain he tried with these and many other words like these, to touch the heart of Minos, inexorable, he was deaf to all his prayers. Seeing his supplications were of no avail, he said to himself, "Behold, here is indeed a chance for thee to prove thy ingenuity. Minos rules the land, and rules the waves, 'tis useless then on sea or land to seek escape. There remains the air, and through the air I'll cleave me a way. Great Jove, pardon the rashness of my under taking. 'Tis not my aim to raise myself to the skyish dwellings of the gods, but there is for me one means, and one alone, whereby I may escape the tyrant. If there were a way across the Styx, the Stygian waters I would not fear to cross. Grant me then to change the laws that rule my nature."

Misfortune ofttimes stimulates invention. Who would ever have thought a man could voyage through the air! Nevertheless, 'tis true that Daedalus wrought himself wings with feathers cunningly disposed like oars, and with thread did fix his flimsy work together. The lower part he bound with wax melted by the fire. And now behold the strange and wondrous work is finished! The boy, with a joyous smile, handles the feathers and the wax, witting not that the wings are destined for his own shoulders. "Behold," cried his father, "the craft that shall bear us to our native land, by its means we shall escape from Minos. Though Minos may have closed all roads to us, he cannot close the highways of the air. Cleave then the air, while still thou mayest, with this my handiwork. But take heed thou draw not too nigh the Virgin of Tegea, or to Orion, who, girt with his sword, doth bear Boötes company. Shape thy course on mine. I will lead the way, be content to follow me, with me to guide thee, thou wilt have nought to fear. For, if in our airy flight we soared too near the sun, the wax of our wings would never bear the heat, and if we flew too low, the moisture of the sea would weight our wings and make them over-heavy for us to move.

Fly then midway between, and O, my son, beware the winds. Whithersoever they may blow, thither let them waft thee." Thus he spake, and fitted the wings upon his son's young shoulders and showed him how to move them, even as the mother bird teaches her feeble fledglings how to fly. That done, he fixes wings on to his own shoulders and half eager, half timid, launches himself on the unfamiliar track. Ere he begins his flight, he kisses his son, and down the old man's cheeks the tears unbidden flow.

Not far from there, stands a hill, which, though less lofty than a mountain, doth yet command the plain. It was from there that they launched themselves on their perilous flight. Daedalus, as he moves his own wings, gazes back at his son's, yet nevertheless keeps steadily on his airy course. At first the novelty of their flight enchants them, and ere long, casting all fear aside, Icarus grows more daring and essays a bolder sweet. A fisherman, about to land a fish with his slender rod, perceives them, and straightway lets it fall. Already they have left Samos behind on the left, and Naxos, and Paros, and Delos dear to Apollo. On their right they have Lebinthos, Calymna shaded with woods, and Astypalaea girdled with pools where fish abound, when lo, young Icarus, growing rash with boyish daring, steers a loftier course and leaves his father. The bonds of his wings relax, the wax melts as the sun grows near, and vainly he waves his arms, they cannot catch the delicate air. Stricken with terror, he looks down from the lofty heavens upon the sea beneath. A darkness born of panic overspreads his eyes. And now the wax has melted, he tosses his naked arms and quakes with fear, for nought is there to upstay him. Down and down he falls, and in his falling cries, "Father, O Father, all is over with me!" And the green waters sealed his mouth for ever. But the unhappy father—a father now no longer cried, "Icarus, where art thou? Beneath what regions of the sky steerest thou thy flight? Icarus, Icarus," he cried and cried again, when lo, on the waste of waters he descried his wings. The land received the bones of Icarus, the sea retains his name.

Minos was powerless to stay a mortal's flight. I am essaying to hold a winged god. If anyone deems there is any virtue in magic or in potions, he sadly errs. Neither the herbs of Medea nor the incantations of the Marsi will make love endure. If there were any potency in magic, Medea would have held the son of Aeson, Circe would have held Ulysses. Philtres, too, that make the face grow pale, are useless when administered to women. They harm the brain and bring on madness. Away with such criminal devices! If you'd be loved, be worthy to be loved. Good looks and a good figure are not enough for that. Though you were Nireus, praised long ago by Homer, ay, were you young Hylas, snatched away by the guilty Naiads, if you would hold your mistress and not one day to be taken aback and find she's left you, add accomplishments of the mind to advantages of the person. Beauty is a fleeting boon, it fades with the passing years, and the longer it lives, the more surely it dies. The violets and wide-cupped lilies bloom not for ever, and once the rose has blown, its naked stem shows only thorns. Thus, my fair youth, thy hair will soon grow white, and wrinkles soon will line thy face with furrows, so set thy beauty off with talents that shall mock at time, 'tis they alone will last unto the grave. Study the refinements of life, and enrich yourself with the treasures of the Greek and Latin tongues. Ulysses was not handsome, but he was eloquent, and two goddesses were tortured with love for him. How often Calypso groaned when she beheld him preparing to depart, and how she kept telling him that the waves would not suffer him to set sail. Times without number she asked him to tell her o'er again the story of the fall of Troy, times without number he would retell it in a new form. One day they were standing on the seashore: the fair nymph was begging him to tell her how the king of Thrace met his cruel death. Ulysses, with a twig which he chanced to have in his hand, drew her a plan upon the sand. "See, here is Troy," he said, tracing the line of the ramparts. "Here runs the Simois. Say this is my camp, farther along is the plain." And he drew it, "which we stained with the blood of Dolon who tried to steal the horses of Achilles by night. There stood the tents of Rhesus, king of Thrace, and it was along there that I rode back with the horses that had been stolen from him." And so he was going on with his narrative, when suddenly a wave came and washed away Troy and Rhesus, together with his camp. Then said the goddess, "Seest thou what famous names these waves have swept away, and dost thou hope they will be kind to thee when thou settest sail?"

Well then, whoever you may be, put not too great a trust in the deceptive charm of beauty. Take care to possess something more than mere physical comeliness. What works wonders with the women is an ingratiating manner. Brusqueness and harsh words only promote dislike. We hate the hawk because it spends its life in fighting, and we hate the wolf that falls upon the timid flocks. But man snares not the swallow because it is gentle, and he suffers the dove to make its home in towers that he has built. Away with all strife and bitterness of speech, pleasant words are the food of love. It is by quarrels that a woman estranges her husband, and a husband estranges his wife. They imagine that in acting so they are paying each other out in their own coin. Leave them to it. Quarrels are the dowry which married folk bring one another. But a mistress should only hear agreeable things. It is not the law that has landed you in bed together. Your law, the law for you and her, is Love. Never approach her but with soft caresses and words that soothe her ear, so that she may always rejoice at your coming.

'Tis is not to the rich that I would teach the art of Love. A man who can give presents has no need of any lessons I can teach him. He has wit enough, and to spare, if he can say when he pleases. "Accept this gift." I give him best. His means are mightier than mine. I am the poor man's poet, because I am poor myself and I have known what it is to be in love. Not being able to pay them in presents, I pay my mistresses in poetry. The poor man must be circumspect in his love-affairs, he mustn't permit himself to use strong language, he must put up with many things that a rich lover would never endure. Once I remember in a fit of ill-temper I ruffled my mistress's hair. It was a fit that robbed me of many and many a happy day. I did not notice that I had torn her dress, and I do not believe I had, but she said I had, and I was obliged to buy her another one. Good friends, be wiser than your master, don't do as he does, or if you do, look out for squalls. Make war on the Parthians to your heart's content, but live at peace with your mistress, have recourse to playfulness and to whatever may excite love.

If your mistress is ungracious and off-hand in her manner towards you, bear it with patience, she'll soon come round. If you bend a branch carefully and gently, it won't break. If you tug at it suddenly with all your might, you'll snap it off. If you let yourself go with the stream, you'll get across the river in time, but if you try to swim against the tide, you'll never do it. Patience will soften tigers and Numidian lions, and slowly and surely you may accustom the bull to the rustic plough. What woman was ever more tameless than Atalanta of Nonacris yet, for all her arrogance, she yielded at length to a lover's tender assiduities. They say that many a time, beneath the trees, Milanion wept at his mishaps and at his mistress's unkindness. Often upon his neck he bore, as he was bid, the treacherous toils, and often with his spear he pierced the savage boars. He was even struck by the arrows of Hylaeus, but other darts, which were, alas, but too well known to him, had dealt him sorer wounds than that.

I do not bid thee climb, armed with thy bow, the woody heights of Maenalus, or carry heavy nets upon thy back. I do not bid thee bare thy breast to a foeman's arrows. If only thou art prudent, thou wilt find my precepts are not over-hard to carry out. If she's obstinate, let her have her way, and you'll get the better of her in the end. Only whatever she tells you to do, be sure you do it. Blame what she blames, like what she likes, say what she says, deny what she denies. If she smiles, smile too, if she sheds tears, shed them too. In a word, model your mood on hers. If she wants to play draughts, play badly on purpose and let her win the game. If you're playing dice, don't let her be piqued at losing, but make it look as though your luck was always out. If your battle-field's the chessboard, see to it that your men of glass are mown down by the foe.

Be sure and hold her parasol over her, and clear a way for her if she's hemmed in by the crowd, fetch a stool to help her on to the couch, and unlace or lace up the sandals on her dainty feet. And then, though you perish with cold yourself, you will often have to warm your mistress's icy hands in your bosom. And you mustn't mind, although it does seem a little undignified, holding up her mirror, like any slave, for her to look in. Why Hercules himself, who performed such mighty feats of bravery and strength, who won a seat in the Olympian realms he had carried on his shoulders, is said to have dwelt among the Ionian maids as one of them, to have held the work-basket and have spun coarse wool. The Tirynthian hero obeyed his mistress's commands, and will you hesitate to endure what he endured?

If your lady-love arranges to meet you in the Forum, be there well before the appointed time, and wait and wait till the very last minute. If she asks you to meet her somewhere else, leave everything and hurry off, don't let the crowd hinder you. If at night, after she's been dining out, she calls a slave to see her home, be quick, offer your services. If you are in the country, and she writes saying, "Come at once." go to her, for Love brooks no delay. If you can't get a conveyance, then you must foot it. Nothing should stop you: thunder, heat, snow, nothing!

Love is like warfare. "Faint heart never won fair lady", poltroons are useless in Love's service. The night, winter, long marches, cruel suffering, painful toil, all these things have to be borne by those who fight in Love's campaigns. Apollo, when he tended the herds of Admetus, dwelt, so 'tis said, in a humble cottage. Who would blush to do as Apollo did? If you would love long and well, you must put away pride. If the ordinary, safe route to your mistress is denied you, if her door is shut against you, climb up on to the roof and let yourself down by the chimney, or the skylight. How it will please her to know the risks you've run for her sake! 'Twill be an earnest of your love. Leander could often have done without his mistress, but he swam the strait to prove his courage.

Nor must you think it beneath your dignity to ingratiate

yourself with her servants, even the humblest of them, greet each of them by name, and take their servile hands in yours. Give them (it will not cost you much) such presents as you can afford, and when the festival of Juno Caprotina comes round, make a handsome present to the lady's-maid. Get on good terms with the occupants of the servants' hall, and don't forget the porter or the slave that sleeps beside your lady's door.

I don't advise you to make costly presents to your mistress, offer her a few trifles, but let them be well chosen and appropriate to the occasion. When the country is displaying all its lavish riches, and the branches of the trees are bending beneath their load, set some young slave to leave a basket of fruit at her door. You can say they come from your place in the country, though in reality you purchased them in Rome. Send her grapes or chestnuts beloved of Amaryllis, though the modern Amaryllis is no longer satisfied with chestnuts. Or again, a present of thrushes or pigeons will prove that you have her still in mind. I know, of course, that this same policy is followed by the expectant legatees of some rich and childless dame. Out on such mean and calculating generosity, say I! Shall I also advise you to send poetry as well? Alas, verses don't count for much. Verses come in for praise, but they really like gifts that are more substantial than that. Even a barbarian, if only he is rich, is sure to find favour. This is the golden age in very truth. Gold will buy the highest honours, and gold will purchase love. Homer himself, even if he came attended by the nine Muses, would promptly be shown the door if he brought no money to recommend him. Nevertheless, there are some cultured women, but they are rare. There are others who are not cultured but who wish to appear so. You must praise them both in your poetry. Whatever the quality of your lines, you may make them sound well if you know how to read them with effect. Indeed, if the lines be well composed and well delivered, the ladies will perhaps deign to regard them as a trifling, a very trifling, present.

Now, when you have determined to do something that you think will be of service, persuade your mistress to ask you to do it. If you have made up your mind to free one of your slaves, see that he addresses his petition to her, if you've resolved not to punish another slave for some neglect of duty, see that it is she who gets the credit for this act of clemency. You'll get the benefit, she'll get the glory. You'll lose nothing, and she'll think she can twist you round her little finger.

If you want to keep your mistress's love, you must make her think you're dazzled with her charms. If she wears a dress of Tyrian purple, tell her there's nothing like Tyrian purple. If she's wearing a gown of Coan stuff, tell her that there's nothing becomes her so enchantingly. If she's ablaze with gold, tell her that you think gold's less brilliant than her charms. If she's clad in winter furs, tell her they're lovely, if she appears in a flimsy tunic, tell her she sets you on fire, and say you hope she won't catch cold. If she wears her hair parted on her forehead, say you like that style. If she has it frizzed and fuzzy, say, "How I love it frizzed!" Praise her arms when she dances, her voice when she sings, and when she ceases, say how sorry you are it came to an end so soon. If she admits you to her bed, adore the seat of all your bliss, and in tones trembling with delight tell her what a heaven she makes for you. Why, even if she were grimmer than the terrible Medusa, she would grow soft and docile for her love. Be a good dissembler and never let your face belie your words. Artifice is a fine thing when it's not perceived, once it's discovered, discomfiture follows. Confidence is gone for ever.

Often when the autumn is at hand, when the earth is adorned with all its charms, when the ruddy grape swells with its purple juice, when we feel alternately a nipping cold or an oppressive heat, this variation of temperature throws us into a state of languor. May your mistress then retain her health. But if some indisposition should compel her to keep her bed, if she falls a victim to the evil effects of the season, then is the time for you to show her how attentive and loving you can be, then is the time to sow the seeds of the harvest you may gather later on. Be not deterred by the attentions her malady demands. Render her whatever services she will deign to accept, let her behold you shedding tears of compassion, never let her see you do not want to kiss her, and let her parched lips be moistened with your tears, say how you hope she'll soon be well again, and be sure to let her hear you saying it, and always be prepared to tell her you have had a dream of happy augury. Let some old grandam, with trembling hands, come and sweeten her bed and purify her room with sulphur and the expiatory eggs. She will store up the memory of these kindnesses in her heart. Many a time have people had legacies bequeathed them for such trifling things as that. But be careful not to display too much anxiety. Do not be over-busy. Your affection and solicitude should have their limits. Don't make it your business to restrict her diet, or tell her she mustn't eat this or that. Don't bring her nasty medicine to drink, leave all that to your rival.

But the wind to which you spread your sails when leaving port is not the wind you need when you are sailing the open sea. Love is delicate at birth, it becomes stronger with use. Feed it with the proper food, and it will grow sturdy in time. The bull that frightens you today, you used to stroke when it was young. The tree that shelters you beneath its shade was once but a frail sapling. A slender rivulet at its source, the river gathers size little by little, and as it flows, is swollen with innumerable tributaries. See to it that thy mistress grows accustomed to thee: nothing is so potent as habit. To win her heart, let no trouble be too great. Let her see you continually, let her hear none but you. Day and night be present to her sight. But when you are sure that she will long for you, then leave her alone, so that your absence may give her some anxiety. Let her repose awhile: the soil that is given a rest renders with usury the seed that's planted in it, and the ground that is parched greedily soaks in the water from the skies. As long as Phyllis had Demophon at her side, her love for him was lukewarm. No sooner had he set sail, than she was consumed with passion for him. Ulysses, shrewd man, tortured Penelope by his absence, and with thy tears, Laodamia, didst thou yearn for the return of Protesilaus.

But be on the safe side, don't stay away too long, time softens the pangs of longing. Out of sight, out of mind. The absent lover is soon forgotten, and another takes his place. When Menelaus had departed, Helen grew weary of her lonely couch and sought warmth and consolation in the arms of her guest. Ah! Menelaus, what a fool wast thou! Alone didst thou depart, leaving thy wife beneath the same roof with a stranger. Fool, 'twas like delivering up the timid dove to the devouring kite, or surrendering the lamb to the hungry wolf. No, Helen was not to blame, her lover was not guilty, she was afraid to lie alone. Let Menelaus think what he will, Helen, in my view, was not to blame, all she did was to profit by her most accommodating husband.

But the fierce boar, in its wildest rage, when, making his last stand, he rolls the fleet hounds over and over, the lioness, when she offers her dugs to the cubs that she is suckling, the viper that the wayfarer has trodden upon with careless foot—all are less redoubtable than the woman who has caught another woman in her husband's bed. Her face is distorted with fury. The sword, the firebrand, anything that comes to her hand, she will seize. Casting all restraint aside, she will rush at her foe like a Maenad driven mad by the Aonian god. The barbarous Medea took vengeance on her own children for Jason's misdeeds and for his violation of the nuptial bond, that swallow that you see yonder was also an unnatural mother. See, her breast still bears the stain of blood. Thus do the happiest, the most firmly welded, unions fail. A cautious lover should beware of exciting these jealous furies.

Do not imagine that I am going to act the rigid moralist and condemn you to love but one mistress. The gods forbid. Even a married woman finds it difficult to keep such a vow as that. Take your fill of amusement, but cast the veil of modesty over your peccadilloes. Never make a parade of your good fortune, and never give a woman a present that another woman will recognise. Vary the time and place of your assignations, lest one of them catch you in some familiar place of rendezvous. When you write, be sure and read over what you have written, many women read into a letter much more than it is intended to convey.

Venus, when she is wounded, justly retaliates, gives the aggressor blow for blow and makes him feel, in his turn, the pain that he has caused. So long as Atridas was satisfied with his wife, she was faithful to him, her husband's infidelity drove her from the narrow path. She learned that Chryses, staff in hand and wearing the sacred fillet on his brows, had begged that his daughter should be restored to him, and begged in vain. She learned, O Briseis, of the abduction that pierced your heart with grief, and for what shameful reasons the war was dragging on. Still all this was only hearsay. But with her own eyes she had seen the daughter of Priam, she had, O sight of shame, seen the victor become the slave of his captive. From that day forth, the daughter of Tyndareus made Aegisthus free of her heart and bed, and took guilty vengeance for her husband's crime. Yet if, how well soever you may hide them, your secret amours come to light, never hesitate to deny your guilt. Be neither sheepish nor gushing, for these are sure signs of a guilty conscience. But spare no effort and employ all your vigour in the battle of love. It's the only way to win peace, the only way to convince her of the unreality of her suspicions. Some people would advise you to stimulate your powers with noxious herbs, such as savory, pepper mixed with thistle-seed or yellow fever-few steeped in old wine. In my view these are nothing more nor less than poisons. The goddess, who dwells on the shady slopes of Mount Eryx, approves not such strained and violent means to the enjoyment of her pleasures. Nevertheless, you may take the white onion that comes from Megara and the stimulating plant that grows in our gardens, together with eggs, honey from Hymettus, and the apples of the lofty pine.

But wherefore, divine Erato, do we wander into these details of the Aesculapian art? Let my chariot return to its own particular track. Awhile ago I was counselling you to hide your infidelities: well, turn about, blazon abroad the conquests you have made. The curved ship is not always obedient to the same wind, she fleets o'er the waves, driven now by the North wind, now by the East. Turn by turn, the West wind and the South will fill her sails. Look at that driver on his chariot there. Sometimes he lets his reins hang loose, sometimes, with skilful hand, he restrains the ardour of his fiery steeds. There are lovers whom a hesitant indulgence ill-befriends. Their mistresses begin to languish if the apprehension of a rival comes not to stimulate their affections. Happiness will sometimes make us drunk and render difficult the way of constancy. A little fire will languish if it be not fed, and disappear beneath the grey ashes that accumulate upon it. But add a little sulphur, and lo, fresh flames will leap and sparkle with new splendour! Thus when the heart grows dull and torpid apply, if you would wake it into life, the spur of jealousy. Give your mistress something to torment her, and bring new heat into her chilly heart. Let her grow pale at the evidence of your inconstancy. What happiness, what untold happiness is his, whose mistress's heart is wrung at the thought of her lover's infidelity. Soon she hears the tidings of his fault, while yet she is fain to hold the news untrue, she swoons and, hapless one, her cheeks grow pale as death, her lips refuse to speak. Oh, would I were that lover! I, whose hair she tears in her wild frenzy, whose face she fiercely scratches with her nails, at whose sight she bursts into floods of tears, but whom she will not, cannot live without! How long, you say, ought one to leave her in despair? Well, hasten to comfort her lest her wrath in the end should harden into bitterness. Hasten to fling thine arms about her snowy neck, and press her tear-stained cheek against thy breast. Kiss away her tears, and with her tears mingle the sweet delights of love. Soon she'll grow calm that is the only way to soothe her wrath. When her rage is at its height, when it is open war between you, then beg her to ratify a peace upon her bed, she'll soon make friends. 'Tis there that, all unarmed, sweet concord dwells, 'tis there, the cradle of forgiveness. The doves that late were fighting, more tenderly will bill and coo, their murmurs seem to tell how true and tender is their love.

Nature, at first, was but a weltering chaos of sky and land and sea. But soon the heavens rose up above the earth, the sea encircled it with a liquid girdle, and from formless chaos issued forth the divers elements. The woods were peopled with wild things, the air with light-winged birds, and the fishes hid themselves beneath the deep waters. In those times men wandered lonely over the face of the earth, and brute strength was their sole resource. The forest was their dwelling-place, the grass was their food, dry leaves was their bed, and for a long time each man dwelt in ignorance of his fellows. Then came the sweet delights of love, and softened, so they say, these rugged hearts, bringing together man and woman on a single couch. No tutor did they need to tell them what to do, Venus, without recourse to any art, fulfilled her gentle office.

The bird has his beloved mate, the fish beneath the waters finds another fish to share his pleasures, the hind follows the stag, the snake mates with the snake, the dog with the bitch, the ewe and the heifer yield themselves with delight to the caresses of the ram and the bull, the goat, noisome though he be, repels not the caresses of his lascivious fellow, the mare, burning with the frenzy of desire, will speed o'er hill and dale, and even through rivers, to join her stallion. Be of good cheer then and employ this potent remedy to calm the anger of thy mistress, 'tis the only sovran cure for her aching sorrow, 'tis a balm sweeter than the juices of Machaon, and if you happen to have erred a little, it will surely bring you pardon.

Such was the burden of my song, when on a sudden Apollo appeared to me and touched with his fingers the chords of a golden lyre, in his hand he bore a branch of laurel, a laurel wreath encircled his brow. Prophetic was his mien and prophetic the voice with which he bade me lead my disciples into his temple. "There," he said, "you will find this inscription famous throughout the whole world, 'Man, know thyself'. The man who knows himself follows ever in his love-affairs the precepts of wisdom. He alone hath wit to adapt his enterprises to his powers. If he is endowed with comely looks, if he has a beautiful skin, let him lie, when he is in bed, with his shoulders uncovered, if he is an attractive talker, let him not maintain a glum silence. If he can sing, let him sing, if the wine makes him merry, let him drink. But whatever he is, orator, babbler, or fine frenzied poet, don't let him interrupt the conversation in order to declaim his prose or his verse." Thus spake Phoebus, and, lovers, you will do well to obey him, nought but the truth ever issued from his god-like lips. But, to my subject, whosoever loves wisely and follows the precepts of my art is sure to conquer and to attain the object of his heart's desire. The furrows do not always repay with interest the seed that has been sown therein, the winds do not always waft the bark-on its uncertain course. Few pleasures, many pains—such is the lot of lovers. Harsh are the trials which they must expect to face. As numerous as the hares on Athos, as the bees on Hybla, as the olives on the tree of Pallas, as the shells upon the seashore, are the sorrows that Love engenders. The arrows he aims at us are steeped in gall. Perhaps they will tell you that your mistress is out, when you know very well she's in, because you've seen her. Never mind, make believe she is out and that your eyes have deceived you. She has promised to let you in at night, and you find her door shut, be patient and lie down on the cold damp ground. Peradventure, some lying servant will come, and looking at you with an insolent stare, say: "What does this fellow want, always besieging our door like this?" Then you must turn the other cheek to this grim seneschal and speak him fair, and not him only, but the door as well, and on the threshold lay the roses that adorned your brow. If your mistress gives you, leave, haste to her side, if she will, none of you withdraw. A well-bred man ought never to make himself a burden. Would you compel her to exclaim: "Is there no way of getting rid of this pestilent fellow?" Women often take unreasonable whims into their head. Never mind, put up with all her insults, never mind if she kicks you even, kiss her dainty feet.

But why linger over such minor details? Let us turn to more important themes. I am going to sing of lofty things. Ye lovers all, lend me your ears. My enterprise is fraught with danger, but without danger, where would courage be? The object I aim at is not easy of attainment. If you have a rival, put up with him without a murmur, and your triumph is assured. You will mount, a conqueror, to Jove's high temple. Believe me, these are not the words of a mere mortal. They are oracles as sure as any that Dodona ever gave. This is the very climax of the art that I impart. If your mistress exchanges meaning glances with your rival—nods and becks and wreathed smiles—put up with it. If she writes him letters, never scrutinise her tablets, let her come and go as she pleases. Hosts of husbands show this indulgence to their lawful wives, especially when thou, soft slumber, aidest in the deceit. Nevertheless, I confess that, in my own case, I cannot attain this degree of perfection. What am I to do? I cannot rise to the height of my own precepts. If I saw a rival making signs to my mistress before my very eyes, do you think I should put up with it, and not give free rein to my wrath? I remember one day her husband kissed her. How I raved and swore about it! Love is made up of these unreasonable demands. This shortcoming has often been my undoing where women are concerned. It is much cleverer of a man to let others have the entree to his mistress. The really proper course is not to know anything about it. Suffer her to hide her infidelities, lest forcing her to confess them should teach her to control her blushes. Ye youthful lovers, then, take heed not to catch your mistresses in the act, lest, while deceiving you they should imagine you were taken in by their fine speeches. Two lovers, who have been found out, do but love each other the more ardently. When, they share a common lot, they both persist in the conduct that brought about their undoing.

There is a story well known throughout Olympus: 'Tis the story of Mars and Venus caught in the act by Vulcan's cunning ruses. Mars, having fallen madly in love with Venus, changed from the grim warrior to the submissive lover. Venus (and never was there a goddess with a heart more tender), Venus showed herself neither awkward nor unfeeling. How many and many a time, they say, the wanton woman laughed at her husband's shambling gait, and at his hands made horny by the heat of the forge and by hard toil. How charming Mars thought her when she imitated the old blacksmith, and how her graceful motions set off her loveliness. To begin with they took the utmost care to conceal their intrigue, and their guilty passion was full of modesty and reserve. But the Sun(nothing ever eludes his glance), the Sun revealed to Vulcan the conduct of his spouse. Ah, Old Sol, what a bad example you set! Demand the favours of the goddess, make her acquiescence the price of your silence, she has the wherewithal to pay you. All around and about his bed Vulcan cunningly stretches a network invisible to every eye. Then he pretends to set out for Lemnos. The two lovers hie them to the familiar spot, and both of them, naked as Cupid himself, are enveloped in the traitorous toils. Then Vulcan calls on the gods to gather round and bids them gaze upon the imprisoned lovers. Venus, so 'tis said, could scarce keep from weeping. They could not hide their faces in their hands, nor cover their nakedness. One of the onlookers thus spoke jeeringly to Mars, "Valiant Mars, quoth he, if thy chains are too heavy for thee, hand them on to me." At length, yielding to the prayers of Neptune, Vulcan set the two captives free. Mars withdrew to Thrace, Venus to Paphos. Say now, Vulcan, what didst thou gain thereby?

Erstwhile they hid their loves, now they freely and openly indulge their passion, they have banished all shame. You'll soon be sorry that you were such a prying fool! Indeed they say that even now you regret that you ever gave way to your anger.

No traps! I forbid you to use them, and Venus herself, who was caught by her spouse, forbids you to make use of tricks, whereof she was the victim. Don't go laying snares for your rival. Don't try and intercept love-letters. Leave such devices, if they think it well to employ them, to lawful husbands whose rights are hallowed by sacred fire and water. As for me, I proclaim it yet again, I only sing of pleasures which the law permits.

Venus herself never putteth off her veil, but with modest hand, she covereth her charms. Who would dare divulge to the profane the mysteries of Ceres and the pious rites instituted in Samothrace? It redounds but little to our credit to keep silence when we are commanded so to do, but to blurt out things we ought to know should be kept secret is a most grievous thing. Rightly was Tantalus punished for his indiscretion, rightly was he debarred from reaching the fruits that hung above his head, it served him right that he should parch with thirst with water all around him. Cytherea, especially, forbids that her mysteries should be revealed. I give thee warning, no babbling knaves should ever draw near her altars. If the sacred emblems of her worship are not concealed in mystic baskets, if no brazen cymbals are beaten at her festivals, if she opens the doors of her temple to all, it is on condition that none shall divulge her mysteries. Venus herself never putteth off her veil, but with modest hand she covereth her charms. The beasts of the field abandon themselves, in any place and in the sight of all, to the delights of love, and often at the spectacle a young girl will turn away her head, but for our loves we must have a secret bower, closed doors, and we must needs cover with vesture the secret places of our body. Even if we seek not for darkness, we like a certain dimness, at all events something a little less than broad daylight. Thus when men and women still went unprotected against the sun and the rain, when the oak provided them with food and shelter, 'twas not in the open, but in caves and woods, that they enjoyed the sweet pleasures of love, so great was the respect which mankind, though still uncouth, entertained for the laws of modesty. Now we make a parade of our nocturnal exploits, and people it seems, would pay a high price for the pleasure of divulging them. Nay, isn't it the fashion nowadays to stop and talk to a girl everywhere one goes, so as to be able to say, "You saw that girl, she's another one I've had!" It's all because they want to have someone to point at, so that every woman who is the object of these attentions becomes the talk of the town. But there's nothing really in it. There are men who invent stories which, if they were true, they would repudiate. To hear them talk, you would think that no woman ever resisted them. If they can't touch their person, they at least attack their good name, and though their body be chaste, their reputation is tarnished. Go, thou hateful warder, and shut the doors upon thy mistress, bolt her in with a hundred bolts. What avail such precautions against the slanderer who brags with lying tongue of the favours he has failed to obtain? Let us, on the other hand, speak sparingly of our real amours, and hide our secret pleasures beneath an impenetrable veil.

Never speak to a woman about her defects, many a lover has had occasion to congratulate himself on having observed this very profitable reticence. The winged-footed hero, Perseus, never found fault with Andromeda for her swarthy skin. Andromache was, in everyone's opinion, far too tall, Hector was the only one who considered her of the average height. Accustom yourself to the things you don't like, you'll learn to put up with them, habit makes a lot of things acceptable. At first, Love will be put off by the merest trifle. A freshly-grafted branch that is just beginning to draw the sap from the green bark will fall off if the slightest breath of wind disturbs it, but if you give it time to grow strong, it will soon resist the winds and, developing into a sturdy branch, enrich the tree that bears it with its alien fruit. Time effaces everything, even bodily defects, and what we once looked upon as blemishes will one day cease to seem so. At first, our nostrils cannot bear the smell of the hides of bulls, they grow used to it in time and bear it without distress.

Moreover, there are words you can employ to palliate defects. If a woman's skin is blacker than Illyrian pitch, tell her she's a brunette. If she squints a little, tell her she's like Venus. If she's carroty, tell her she's like Minerva. If she's so skinny you would think she was at death's door, tell her she has a graceful figure. If she's short, so much the better, she's all the lighter. If she's thick-waisted, why she's just agreeably plump. Similarly, you must disguise every defect under the name of its nearest quality. Never ask her how old she is, or who was consul when she was born. Leave it to the Censor to perform that uncomfortable duty, especially if she has passed the flower of her youth, if the summer of her days is over, and if she is already compelled to pull out her grey hairs. My young friends, that age, and even an older one than that, is not without its pleasures. It is a field that you should sow and one day You will reap your harvest. Labour while your strength and your youth allow. All too soon tottering eld, with noiseless tread, will be upon you. Cleave the waters of the ocean with your oar, or the glebe with your slough, wield with warlike arm the deadly sword, or devote to women your vigour and your care. 'Tis but another kind of military service, and in it too, rich trophies may be won.

Nor should it be forgotten that women, who are getting on in years, have experience, and it is only experience that sets the seal of perfection on our natural gifts. They repair by their toilet the ravages of time, and by the care they take of themselves manage to conceal their age. They know all the different attitudes of Love and will assume them at your pleasure. No pictured representation can rival them in voluptuousness. With them pleasure comes naturally, without provocation, the pleasure which is sweeter than all, the pleasure which is shared equally by the man and the woman. I hate those embraces in which both do not consummate, that is why boys please me but little. I hate a woman who offers herself because she ought to do so, and cold and dry, thinks of her sewing when she's making love. The pleasure that is granted to me from a sense of duty ceases to be a pleasure at all. I won't have any woman doing her duty towards me. How sweet it is to hear her voice quaver as she tells me the joy she feels, and to hear her imploring me to slacken my speed so as to prolong her bliss. How I love to see her, drunk with delight, gazing with swooning eyes upon me or languishing with love, keeping me a long while at arms' length.

But these accomplishments are not vouchsafed by nature to young girls. They are reserved for women who have passed the age of thirty-five. Let who will hasten to drink new and immature wine. Let me have a rich mellow vintage dating back to one of our elder consuls. It is only after many years that the plane tree affords a shelter from the scorching sun, and fields but newly reaped hurt the naked foot. What! Do you mean to tell me you would put Hermione before Helen? And would Althaea's daughter outrival her mother? If you would enjoy the fruits of love in their maturity, you will obtain, if only you persevere, a reward worthy of your desires.

But already the bed, the minister of their pleasures, has received our two lovers. Stay thy steps, my Muse, at the closed door. They will know well enough, without thy aid, what words to say to one another, and their hands within the bed will not be idle. Their fingers will find the way to those secret places in which Love is wont to proclaim his presence. 'Twas even thus that the valiant Hector, whose skill was not confined to battle, bore himself with Andromache. Thus too the great Achilles fondled his fair captive when, weary of fighting, he lay beside her on the downy couch. Thou didst not fear, Briseis, to yield thyself to the caresses of those hands that bore upon them still the stains of Trojan blood. Was there ought to compare, voluptuous girl, with the pleasure of feeling the pressure of those victorious hands?

If you listen to my advice, you will not be in too great a hurry to attain the limits of your pleasure. Learn by skilful dallying, to reach the goal by gentle, pleasant stages. When you have found the sanctuary of bliss, let no foolish modesty arrest your hand. Then will you see the love-light trembling in her eyes, even as the rays of the sun sparkle on the dancing waves. Then will follow gentle moanings mingled with murmurings of love, soft groans and sighs and whispered words that sting and lash desire. But now beware! Take heed lest, cramming on too much sail, you speed too swiftly for your mistress. Nor should you suffer her to outstrip you. Speed on together towards the promised haven. The height of bliss is reached when, unable any longer to withstand the wave of pleasure, lover and mistress at one and the same moment are overcome. Such should be thy rule when time is yours and fear does not compel you to hasten your stolen pleasures. Nevertheless, if there be danger in delay, lean well forward, and drive your spur deep into your courser's side.

My task draws toward its end. Young lovers show your gratitude. Give me the palm and wreathe my brow with the fragrant myrtle. As Podalirius was famous among the Greeks for his skill in curing disease, Pyrrhus for his valour, Nestor for his eloquence, as Calchas was famed for his skill in foretelling the future, Telamon for wielding weapons, Automedon for chariot-racing, so do I excel in the art of Love. Lovers, laud your Poet, sing my praises, so that my name may resound throughout the world. I have given you arms. Vulcan gave arms to Achilles. With them he was victorious. Learn ye too to conquer with mine. And let every lover, who shall have triumphed over a doughty Amazon with the sword I gave him, inscribe on his trophies, "Ovid was my Master."

But now the girls, look you, want me to give them some lessons. You, my dears, shall be my instant care.

BOOK III
On Winning and Holding Love

I have just armed the Greeks against the Amazons, now, Penthesilea, it remains for me to arm thee against the Greeks, thee and thy valiant troop. Fight with equal resources and let the victory go to he side favoured by beloved Dione and the boy who flies over the whole world. It was not right to expose you, all defenceless as you were, to the attacks of a well-armed foe. Victory, my men, at such a price as that would be a disgrace.

But perchance one among you will say to me, "Wherefore give fresh poison to the snake, wherefore surrender the lamb to the raging wolf?" Now forbear to condemn the whole sex for the crimes of a few of its members, let every woman be judged on her own merits. If the young Alcides had reason to complain of Helen, if his elder brother could with justice accuse Clytemnestra, Helen's sister, if through the crime of Eriphyle, the daughter of Talaus, Amphiaraus went riding to the under-world on his living steeds, is it not also true that Penelope remained chaste when sundered from her husband who was kept for ten years fighting before Troy and who, when Troy had fallen, wandered over the seas for ten years more? Look at Laodamia, who, in order to join her husband in the grave, died long before her tale of years was told. And Alcestis, who, by sacrificing her own life, redeemed her husband, Admetus, from the tomb. "Take me in thine arms, Capaneus, and let our ashes at least be mingled." exclaimed the daughter of Iphis, and forthwith leapt into the midst of the pyre.

Virtue is a woman both in vesture and in name, what wonder, therefore, that she should favour her own sex? Nevertheless, it is not these lofty souls that my art requires, lighter sails are suited to my pinnace. Only wanton loves are the burden of my discourse, to women I am about to teach the art of making themselves beloved.

Woman cannot resist the flames and cruel darts of love, shafts which, methinks, pierce not the heart of man so deeply. Man is ever a deceiver, woman deceives but rarely. Make a study of women, you'll find but few unfaithful ones among them. False Jason cast off Medea when she was already a mother, and took another woman to his arms. It is no thanks to thee, O Theseus, that Ariadne, abandoned on an unknown shore, fell not a prey to the birds of the sea.

Wherefore did Phyllis return nine times to the seashore? Ask that question of the woods, who, in sorrow for her loss, shed their green raiment. Thy guest, Dido, for all his much-belauded conscience, fled from thee, leaving thee, nought save the sword that brought thee death. Ah, hapless ones, shall I reveal to you the cause of your undoing? You knew not how to love. You lacked the art, and art makes love endure. And even now they would still continue in their ignorance, but that Cytherea bids me instruct them. Into my presence did Cytherea come and thus she did command. "What ill, then, have they wrought thee, these unhappy women, that thou deliverest them, all defenceless as they are, into the hands of the men whom thou thyself hast armed? Thou hast devoted two poems to instructing men. And now the women in their turn demand thy aid. The poet who had outpoured the vials of his scorn on the wife of Menelaus, soon repented, and sang her praises in a palinode. If I know thee truly, thou art not the man to be unkind to the women. Thou wouldst rather seek to serve them so long as thou dost live." Thus she spake, and from the wreath that crowned her hair, she took a leaf and a few myrtle berries, which she gave to me. As I took them, an influence divine was shed about me. The air shone purer round about me, and it seemed as though a burden had been lifted from my heart.

While Venus inspires me, my fair ones, give ear unto my counsel. Modesty and the law and your privileges permit. Bethink you, then, of old age which cometh all too soon, and not an instant will you lose. While yet you may, and while you yet enjoy the spring-time of your years, taste of the sweets of life. The years flow on like to the waters of a river. The stream that fleeteth by, never returns to the source whence it sprang. The hour that hath sped returns again no more. Make the most of your youth, youth that flies apace. Each new day that dawn is less sweet than those which went before. Here, where the land is rough with withering bracken, I have seen the violet bloom, from this thorny bush, I once did wreathe me garlands of roses. Thou who rejectest love, today art but a girl, but the time will come when, all alone and old, thou wilt shiver with cold through the long dark hours in thy solitary bed. No more shall rival swains come of a night and, battling for your favours, batter down your doors, no more, of a morning, will you find your threshold strewn with roses. Ah me! How soon the wrinkles come, how swiftly fades the colour from the beauteous cheek! Those white hairs, which (so at least you swear) you had when you were quite a child, will swiftly cover all your head. The snake, when he sloughs off his skin, sloughs off the burden of his years, and the stag, when he sprouts new horns, renews his youth. But nothing brings amends for what Time filches from us. Pluck, then, the rose and lose no time, since if thou pluck it not 'twill fall forlorn and withered, of its own accord. Besides, the toil of child-bearing shortens the span of youth, too frequent harvests make the soil wax old. Blush not, O Phoebe, that thou didst love Endymion upon the Latmian height. And Dawn, thou goddess of the rosy fingers, that thou didst bear off Cephalus, was no shame to thee Nay, though of Adonis we refrain to speak, whom Venus still doth mourn today, to whom, if not to love, owed she Aeneas and Hermione? Follow then, ye mortal maidens, in the footsteps of these goddesses, withhold not your favours from your ardent lovers.

If they deceive you, wherein is your loss? All your charms remain, and even if a thousand should partake of them, those charms would still be unimpaired. Iron and stone will wear thin by rubbing, that precious part of you defies attrition, and you need never fear 'twill wear away. Doth a torch lose aught of its brightness by giving flame to another torch? Should we fear to take water from the mighty ocean? "A woman," you will say, "ought not thus to give herself to a man." Come now, why not? What does she lose? Nought but the liquid which she may take in again at will. Ah, no! I am not telling you to make drabs of yourselves, but merely not to be scared of some imaginary ill, the bestowal of such gifts will never make you poor.

But I am still within the harbour. A gentle breeze will waft me to the main. Once well out on the open sea, I shall be borne along by a stronger wind. Let me begin with dress. A well-tended vine yields a good harvest, and high stands the corn on the well-tilled field. Good looks are the gift of God, but how few can pride themselves upon their beauty. The majority of you have not been vouchsafed this favour. A careful toilet will make you attractive, but without such attention, the loveliest faces lose their charm, even were they comparable to those of the Idalian goddess herself. If the beautiful women of ancient times recked not of their appearance, the men were not a whit less careless.

If Andromache arrayed herself in a coarse tunic, why should we marvel? She was the wife of a rugged soldier. Would the wife of Ajax come richly apparelled to a warrior clad in the hides of seven oxen? In those far-off days, the ways of our forefathers were rude and simple. Rome nowadays is all ablaze with gold, rich with the wealth of the world that she hath conquered. Look at the Capitol, compare it now with what it once was. You would say it was a temple consecrated to another Jupiter. The palace of the Senate, worthy now of the august assembly that sits within it was in the days when Tatius was king, nothing but a thatched cottage. These gorgeous edifices on the Palatine Hill, built in honour of Apollo and our great leaders, were once but pasture ground for oxen that dragged the plough. Let others belaud those ancient times, I am satisfied to be a child of today. I find it better suited to my tastes, not because nowadays we ransack the bowels of the earth for gold, and import purple dyes from distant shores, not because we see the mountains shrink because we are eternally quarrying them for marble, not because vast moles keep far away the billows of the deep, but because we enjoy the amenities of life, and because those rough and boorish ways, which for a long time characterised our ancestors, have not endured to our day.

Nevertheless, burden not your ears with those sumptuous pearls which the dusky Indian seeks beneath the green waves. Go not forth in garments heavily inwrought with gold. The wealth by which you would fain attract us, very often just repels us. Neatness is what we like. Let your hair be nicely done. That depends greatly on the skill of the person that dresses it. Of course there are innumerable ways of doing it. Every woman should study to find out the style that suits her best, and for that her mirror is the surest guide! Long features demand that the hair should be simply parted on the forehead. Such was the style of Laodamia. Women with round faces should wear their hair lightly twisted into a knot on the top of the head, leaving the ears exposed. One woman will let her hair fall loose on either shoulder, like Apollo when he holds his dulcet lyre. Another must needs have her hair tied up behind, like

Diana when she pursueth the wild beasts in the forests. One delights us with her loose flowing ringlets, another by wearing her hair closely patted down upon her temples. Some women like to adorn their hair with the shell of the Cyllenian tortoise, others to wear it in towering waves. But there are not more acorns on an oak tree, more bees on Hybla, or wild beasts on the mountains, than there are modes of doing a woman's hair, and new ones are invented every day. Some women look well with their hair done in careless fashion: you might think it hadn't been done since yesterday. In point of fact it has only just been combed. Artifice should look like carelessness. Such was Iole when Hercules first saw her in the captured city. "That is the woman for me." he exclaimed. Such, too, was Ariadne, forsaken on the shores of Naxos, when Bacchus bore her away in his chariot, while the Satyrs cried *"Evoë"*. Ah, you women! Nature, kindly toward your charms, has given you how many means to repair the ravages of time! We men, alas, grow bald. Our hair, of which time robs us, falls even as the leaves when the North wind brings them down. A woman will dye her hair with the juice of some German herb, and the artificial colour becomes her better than the natural one. A woman will appear wearing a mass of hair that she has just purchased. For a little money she can buy another's tresses. She'll do the deal without a blush, quite openly, in front of Hercules and the Virgin band.

Now what shall I say about clothes? I care not for those golden flounces, or wool twice dipped in Tyrian purple? There are so many other colours that cost less money. Why carry all your fortune on your back? Look at this azure blue like a clear sky when the wind has ceased to herd the rain clouds from the South. Now look, too, at this golden yellow, 'tis the colour of the ram which once on a time saved Phryxus and Helle from the snares of Ino. That green is called water-green from the colour that it imitates, I could easily imagine that the Nymphs were clothed in such apparel. This hue resembles saffron, it is the colour wherein. Aurora arrays herself when, moist with dew, she yokes her shining coursers to her car. There you will recognise the colour of the myrtle of Paphos, here the purple amethyst, the whitening rose, or the Thracian stork, and here again the colour of thy chestnuts, Amaryllis, or thy almonds, or the colour of that stuff to which wax has given its name. As numerous as the flowers which blow when sluggish Winter hath departed, and when beneath the Spring's soft breath, the vine puts forth its buds, so many and more are the hues that wool receives from all its many dyes. Choose then with care, for all colours are not becoming to all people. Black suits a fair complexion: it became Briseis, she was dressed in black when she was carried off.

White suits dark people, white, Andromeda, set off your charms, and 'twas white that you were wearing when you set foot on the isle of Seriphos.

I was going to tell you not to let your armpits smell, and to see that your legs were not rough with bristles. But it's not, of course, to the coarse Caucasian women I am addressing my remarks, nor yet to the women who drink the waters of the Caicus. I need not tell you never to neglect to keep your teeth white and to rinse your mouth out every morning with clean water. With wax you know how to whiten your skin, and with carmine to give yourself the rosy hue which Nature has denied you. Your art will tell you how to fill the space between your eyebrows, if it be too, faintly marked, and how, with cosmetics, to conceal the all too patent evidence of the growing years. You fear not to increase the brightness of your eyes with finely powdered ash, or with the saffron that grows on the banks of the Cydnus. I have told of the ways of restoring beauty in a work, which though slender, is of great value by reason of the studied care with which I wrote it. Consult it for the remedies you need, all you young women on whom Nature has not lavished her favours. You will find my treatise abounds in useful counsel.

But on no account let your lover find you with a lot of "aids to beauty" boxes about you. The art that adorns you should be unsuspected. Who but would feel a sensation of disgust if the paint on your face were so thick that it oozed down on to your breasts? What words could describe the sickening smell of the oesypum although it comes from Athens, that oily juice which they extract from the fleece of sheep. I should also disapprove of your using stag's marrow, or of your cleaning your teeth when anyone is there to see. I know all that would enhance your charms, but the sight would be none the less disagreeable. How many things revolt us in the process, which delight us in the achievement. Those famous masterpieces of the sculptor Myron were once but useless, shapeless blocks of marble. If you want a ring of gold, you've got to hammer it into shape, the material you wear was once dirty, evil-smelling wool. That marble, once an unhewn block, is now a masterpiece—Venus, naked, wringing the water from her dripping hair. Let your servants tell us you are still asleep, if we arrive before your toilet's finished. You will appear all the lovelier when you've put on the finishing touch. Why should I know what it is that makes your skin so white? Keep your door shut, and don't let me see the work before it's finished. There are a whole host of things we men should know nothing about. Most of these various artifices would give us a nasty turn, if you didn't take care not to let us see them. Look at those brilliant ornaments that adorn the stage.

If you examined them closely, you would see that they are merely gilded wood. None of the audience are allowed to go near till everything is finished and in order. Just in the same way, it's only when the men are away that you ought to do your titivating.

Howbeit, I do not by any means forbid you to comb your hair before us, I love to see it fall in floating tresses about your shoulders. But never get vexed or petulant, and don't keep on fidgeting with your curls. Don't treat your maid so as to make her in terror of you. I detest the sort of shrew that scratches her maid's face, or sticks a needle in her arm, in a fit of temper. It makes the poor girl wish the devil would take the head she is holding between her hands, and with blood and tears she moistens her mistress's hateful tresses. Every woman who has but little hair should have a sentinel at her door, or else always have her hair attended to in the temple of the Bona Dea. One day I was announced unexpectedly to my mistress, and in her flurry she put on her false hair all awry. May such a mischance never befall any but our enemies! May such a disgrace be reserved for the daughters of the Parthians. A mutilated animal, a barren field, a leafless tree are hideous things to see: a bald head is not less so.

'Tis not to you, Semele or Leda, that I address my lessons, nor to thee, O fair Sidonian, who wast borne by a fictitious bull across the seas, nor yet to Helen whom thou with reason, Menelaus, didst demand, and whom thou, her ravisher, did with equal reason refuse to give up. My host of pupils is composed of fair women and of plain, and these latter always outnumber the rest. The pretty ones are less in need of art's assistance and take its admonitions less to heart, they are the fortunate possessors of charms whose potency owes nought to art. When the sea is calm, the mariner lays him down to rest in careless ease, when the tempest sets it on a roar, he quits not his station even for an instant.

Rare, however, is the face without a fault. Hide these blemishes with care, and so far as may be, conceal the defects of your figure. If you are short, sit down, lest when standing you should be thought to be sitting, if you are a dwarf, lie stretched at full length on your couch, and so that none may see how short you are, throw something over your feet to hide them. If you are thin, wear dresses of thick material and have a mantle hanging loosely about your shoulders. If you are sallow, put on a little rouge, if you are swarthy, see what the fish of Pharos will do for you. Let an ungainly foot be hid in a white leathern shoe. If your legs are thin, don't be seen unlacing your sandals. If your shoulder-blades are prominent, little pads will correct the defect. If you have too full a bust, contain it with a brassière. If your fingers are stumpy and your nails unsightly, don't gesticulate when you are talking. If your breath is strong, you should never talk when your stomach's empty, and always keep some distance away from your lover. A woman whose teeth are discoloured, or prominent, or uneven, will often give herself away when she laughs. Who would imagine it? Women are even taught how to laugh. Even in such a detail as that, they study to be charming. Don't open your mouth too wide, let the dimples on either side be small, and let the extremity of the lips cover the upper part of the teeth. Don't laugh too often and too loud. Let there be something feminine and gentle in your laughter, something agreeable to the ear. Some women cannot laugh without making a hideous grimace, others try to show how pleased they are, and you would imagine they were crying, others offend the car with harsh and ugly sounds, like the noise a dirty old she-ass makes as she brays at the mill-stone.

Where indeed does Art not have a say! Why, women even learn to weep gracefully, to cry when they will, and as much as they will. And then there are women who don't pronounce a certain letter in their words, and lisp with affectation when they come to it. This assumed defect lends them an added charm, so they actually practise speaking imperfectly. All these, are details, but, since they have their uses, practise them assiduously. Learn also how to walk as a woman should. There is a style in walking that should be carefully cultivated, and that style, or the lack of it, will often attract or repel a stranger. This woman, for example, walks with an elegant swing from the hips, her gown floats gracefully in the breeze, and she moves with dignity and charm. And here again is a woman who elbows her way along with huge strides like the red-faced wife of an Umbrian peasant. But in this matter of walking, as in everything else, we must have a sense of proportion. One woman will walk too much like a country wench, another with over-much mincing and affectation. Then, again, you should leave uncovered the top of your shoulder and the upper part of your left arm. That is especially becoming to women who have a white skin. At the mere sight of it, I should be mad to cover all I could touch with kisses.

The Sirens were monsters of the deep, and, with their wondrous singing, stayed the swiftest vessels in their flight. When their song fell upon his ears, Ulysses was sore tempted to unbind himself from the mast, as for his companions, their ears were stopped with wax. Music is a soothing thing. Women should learn to sing. Many a woman has made up for her lack of beauty by the sweetness of her voice. Sometimes sing over the songs you have heard at the theatre, sometimes sing voluptuous, Oriental airs. A woman, who is fain to attract, should know how to play the lute and the harp. Thracian Orpheus, with his lyre, charmed rocks and wild beasts, aye, and Acheron and the triple-headed Cerberus. And thou, Amphion, righteous avenger of thy mother's wrong, didst thou not behold stones rise up at the sound of thy voice and range themselves into walls? Who has not heard of the wonders wrought by Arion with his lyre? Even the dumb fish is said to have listened, enchanted, to his song. Learn, too, to sweep the strings of the joyous psaltery with either hand. 'Tis an instrument favourable to the dalliance of lovers. You should also learn Callimachus by heart, and Philetas and Anacreon, who loved his drop of wine. And Sappho too, for what is more exciting than her verse? Then there's the poet who tells us about a father being hoodwinked by the crafty Geta. You might also read the verses of the tender-souled Propertius, and the poems of my beloved Tibullus, and something out of Gallus, or the poem Varro wrote about the golden fleece so bitterly lamented, Phrixus, by thy sister, and the story of the fugitive, Aeneas, and the origins of lofty Rome, for Latium boasts no prouder masterpiece than that. And peradventure shall my name with theirs be numbered, and my writings shall not be given over to the waters of Lethe, and perchance someone will say, "Read o'er these dainty lines wherein our Master gives instruction both to men and women, or choose, in those three books, the which he calls the

Loves, passages which you will read with sweetly modulated voice, or, if thou wilt, declaim with skill one of those letters from his Heroines, a kind of work unknown before his time and whereof he himself was the inventor." Hear my prayers, O Phoebus, hear them, mighty Bacchus, and you, ye Muses, divine protectresses of poets.

Who could doubt that I want my charmer to be skilled in the dance? I would that, when the wine-cup is placed upon the table, she should be accomplished in swaying her arms to the measure of the music. Graceful dancers delight your theatre-goer. Such grace, such airy lightness, charms us all.

I am loth to enter into petty details, but I should like my pupil to know how to throw the dice with skill, and to calculate with nicety the impetus she gives them as she tosses them on to the table. I should like her to know when to throw the three numbers, and when to take and when to call. I should wish her to play chess with skill and caution. One piece against two is bound to go under. A king that is battling, separated from his queen is liable to be taken, and his rival is often compelled to retrace his steps. Again, when the ball bounces against the broad racquet, you must only touch the one you intend to serve. There is another game divided into as many parts as there are months in the year. A table has three pieces on either side, the winner must get all the pieces in a straight line. It is a bad thing for a woman not to know how to play, for love often comes into being during play.

Still, it is only half the battle merely to play well, the important thing is to be master of yourself. Sometimes, when we are not properly on our guard, when we are carried away by the heat of the game, we forget ourselves and let our inmost nature stand revealed. Rage and love of gain, such are the shameful vices that lay hold on us, thence spring quarrels, brawls and vain regrets. Hot words are bandied to and fro, the air resounds with angry shouts, and each one calls in turn on the wrathful gods for help. Then no player trusts another, "The pieces have been tampered with." they cry, and to have fresh ones they insist, and many a time, I've seen their faces bathed with tears. May Jove preserve us from tantrums such as that, any woman who aims at pleasing us.

Such are the games which kindly Nature to your weakness doth vouchsafe. To man she opens forth an ampler field: to him the flying ball, the spear, the quoit and daring feats of horsemanship. You are not made to strive in contests on the field of Mars, or to plunge into the icy waters of the Virgin's spring, or into the tranquil current of the Tiber. But you may, and you would do well to do so, walk in the shade of Pompey's Portico when the fiery coursers of the Sun are entering the constellation of Virgo. Visit the temple sacred to Apollo, to the god whose brow is decked with the laurel, and who, at Actium, whelmed the Egyptian fleet beneath the wave, visit those stately buildings raised by the sister and wife of Augustus, and his son-in-law decorated with the naval crown. Draw near to the altars where incense is offered to the sacred cow of Memphis, visit our three theatres, splendid places for displaying your attractions, go to the arena still warm with blood new-shed, and that goal round which the chariots whirl with fiery wheel.

Things that are hidden no one heeds, and none desires what he has never known. What avails a beautiful face if none be there to see it? Even though you should sing songs more sweet than the songs of Thamyris and Amoebeus, who would praise the merits of your lyre, if there were none to hear it? If Apelles, of Cos, had not given us his vision of Venus, the goddess would still be buried beneath the waves. What does the poet long for? He longs for fame. That is the guerdon we look for to crown our toil. Time was when poets were the favourites of heroes and of kings, and in ancient days a choir of singers gained a rich reward. Hallowed was the dignity and venerable the name of Poet, and upon them great riches were often bestowed. Ennius, born in the mountains of Calabria, was deemed worthy of being buried nigh to thee, great Scipio. But now the poet's crown of ivy lies unhonoured, and they, who through the hours of night do strictly meditate the Muse, are idlers held. Howbeit, they strive, and love to strive, for fame. Who would have heard of Homer if the *Iliad*—the deathless *Iliad*—had never seen the light? Who would have known Danaë, if for ever a prisoner, she had languished till old age came upon her in her tower?

You, my fair young charmers, will do well to mingle with the throng, bend your roaming footsteps full oft beyond your thresholds. The she-wolf has her eye on many a sheep before she selects her prey, the eagle pursues more birds than one. Thus a pretty girl should show herself in public. In the throng there is perhaps one lover in whom her charms will strike an answering chord. Wherever she be, let her show herself eager to please, and let her be mindful of everything that could enhance her charms. You never know when a chance may occur. Always have the bait ready. The fish will come and bite when you least expect it. It often happens that the dogs scour the woods and hills in vain, and then the stag comes of his own accord, and steps into the net. When Andromeda was chained to her rock, how was she to hope that anyone should have compassion on her tears? Often a new husband is discovered at the old one's funeral: nothing makes a woman so alluring as to walk with dishevelled hair and let her tears flow unrestrainedly.

But avoid the man that makes a parade of his clothes and his good looks, and is on the tenterhooks lest his hair should get ruffled. The sort of thing such men will tell you, they've said over and over again to other women. They're of the roving sort and never settle anywhere. What can a woman do when a man is more of a woman than she is, and perhaps has a bigger following of lovers? Perhaps you won't believe this, and yet it's perfectly true: Troy would still be standing, if the Trojans had listened to old Priam's advice. There are men who get on good terms with women by making out they love them, and having done so, proceed disgracefully to fleece them. Don't be taken in by their scented locks, their dandified clothes, their affected aestheticism, and their much-beringed fingers. Perhaps the smartest of all these fine gentlemen is nothing but a crook, whose sole aim is to rob you of your fine clothes. "Give me back my property" is the burden of many a poor woman's complaint, whom some such ruffian has taken in. "Give me back my property" is what you are always hearing in every court of justice. And you, O Venus, and you, ye goddesses, whose temples grace the Appian Way, look down upon the scene unmoved. And some there are among these rakes, whose reputation is so blown upon, that any women who are taken in by them deserve no sympathy.

Women, learn from the misfortunes of others, how to avoid a similar fate, and never let your door give admittance to a swindler. Beware, ye daughters of Cecrops, of paying heed to the protestations of Theseus! It wouldn't be the first time he had taken his solemn oath to a lie. And you, Demophon, who inherited Theseus' gift for lying, how we can trust you, seeing how you broke your vows to Phyllis! If, my dears, your lovers bring you glittering promises, do the like to them, if they bring you presents, let them have the favours they have bargained for. A woman who, after receiving presents from her lover, withholds from him the pleasure that he has a right to, would be capable of extinguishing Vesta's eternal flame, of stealing the sacred vessels from the temple of Inachus, and of sending her husband to his last account with a glass of aconite and hemlock.

But come now, where am I getting to? Come, my Muse, draw in your reins a little, lest your steeds carry me beyond my goal. When your lover has paved the way with a brief note or two, and when your wide-awake maid has duly received and delivered them, read them over very carefully, weigh every word, and try to find out whether his love is merely pretence or whether he really means what he says. Don't be in too great a hurry to answer him, suspense, if it be not too prolonged, acts as a spur to love. Don't appear too accommodating to him, if he's a youngster, on the other hand, don't rap him too severely over the knuckles. Act in such a way as to instil him at once with hope and fear, and every time you say "No" make him think he'll have a better chance next time. What you write him should be ladylike, but simple and direct. Ordinary, unaffected language pleases the most. It often happens that a letter gives the necessary impulse to a hesitating heart, and how often too has some clumsy uncouth utterance completely neutralised a girl's good looks.

But you women who, though you don't aim at the honours of chastity, want to cuckold your husbands without their knowing it, be sure not to send your letters by any but a trusty hand. On no account send these evidences of your passion to an inexperienced lover. For failing to observe this precaution, I have seen young married women white with fear and spending their unhappy days in a condition of continuous slavery.

Doubtless it is a shame for a man to keep such damning proofs, but they put into his hands weapons as terrible as the fires of Etna. In my idea, deceit should be countered by deceit, just as the law allows us to repel violence by violence. You should practise varying your handwriting as much as possible. Foul fall the knaves that compel me to give you such advice. And you should be sure and not write on a tablet that has been used, without making quite sure that the original writing has been quite rubbed out, lest the wax should give evidence of two different hands. The letters you write to your lover should be addressed as though to a woman, and you should always allude to him as her.

But let us leave these minor details for graver subjects, let us cram on all sail. If you want to retain your good looks, you must restrain your temper. Peace, gentle peace, is the attribute of man, as rage and fury are the characteristics of wild beasts. Rage puffs out the face, gorges the veins with blood, and kindles in the eye the fiery fury of the Gorgon. "Away with thee, miserable flute, thou deservest not that I should spoil my beauty for thee." said Pallas, when in the stream she beheld her distorted visage. And so with you. If any of you women looked at yourselves in the glass when you were in a raging temper, you wouldn't know yourselves, not one of you! Another thing, just as unbecoming, is pride. You must have a soft, appealing expression, if you want to attract a lover. Believe an old hand at the game. A haughty, disdainful look puts a man out of tune at once, and sometimes, even though a woman doesn't say a word, her countenance betrays something hostile and disagreeable. Look at whoever looks at you, smile back when you're smiled at, if anyone makes signs to you, send back an answering signal. 'Tis thus that love, after making essay with harmless arrows, draws from his quiver his pointed darts. We also dislike gloomy women. Let Ajax love his Tecmessa. We are a jovial company, and we like a woman to be gay. As for you, Andromache, and you, Tecmessa, I should never have wanted either of you for a mistress, and beyond mere child-getting, I doubt whether your husbands sought, or found, any great pleasure within your arms. How can we imagine so dreary a woman as Tecmessa ever saying to Ajax, "O Light of my life" and all those other sweet things that charm us and console.

Let me be suffered to illustrate my own gay trifling art with examples from a much more serious affair. Let me compare it to the tactics of a general commanding an army. A leader that knows his business will entrust, to one officer the command of a hundred infantrymen, to another a squadron of cavalry, to another, the standards. Now you women should consider in what respect we can serve you best, and assign to each of us his special part. If a man's rich, make him give you presents, let the legal luminary give you his professional advice, let the eloquent barrister plead his lovely client's cause. As for us poets, we've got nothing to offer you but our verses, but what we can do better than the rest of them is to love, and we spread far and wide the renown of the charmer that has succeeded in captivating us. Nemesis and Cynthia are famous names, Lycoris from East to West is known, and now on every hand they want to know who is this Corinna that I sing about. Perjury is hateful to a poet, and poetry too is a great factor in the making of a gentleman. Ambition, love of riches, these things torment us not, we reck not of the Forum and its triumphs, all we seek is seclusion and repose. Love is swift to take hold of us and burns us with its fiercest flame, and into our love, alas, we put over-much of trust and confidence.

The peaceful art which we pursue lends a softness to our manners, and our mode of life is consonant with our work. My fair ones, never withhold your favours, from the poets, the gods inspire them and the Muses smile upon them. Ay, a god dwells within us and we commerce with the skies. From the high heavens doth our inspiration come. How shameful to expect hard cash from a poet, yet it's a shame no pretty woman is afraid to incur.

Learn how to dissemble, and don't display your avarice all at once. Mind you don't lose a fresh lover when he realises the trap you are laying for him. A skilful groom doesn't treat a colt just broken like a horse that has grown used to harness. In the same way, you won't catch a novice with the same snare as you use for a veteran. The one, a new recruit, is fighting for the first time in his life beneath the standards of love, he has never before been captured, and now that you have snared him, you must let him know none but you. He is like a young sapling, and you must surround him with a lofty fence. Be sure to keep all possible rivals out of the way. You will only retain your conquest if you share it with no one. Love's dominion, like a king's, admits of no partition. So much for the novice, the other is an old campaigner. His pace is slower and more deliberate. He will endure many things that a raw recruit could never stand. He won't come battering in or burning down your front door. He won't scratch and tear his sweetheart's dainty check till the blood comes. He won't rend his garments, or hers either, he won't pull her hair out and make her cry. Such tantrums as that are only permitted in youngsters, in the heyday of youth and heat. But your older man is not a bit like that. He'll put up with all manner of snubs. He smoulders with a small fire like a damp torch or like green wood fresh hewn on the mountain top. His love is more sure, the other's is more blithe, but it doesn't last so long. Be quick and pluck the fleeting blossom. Well, let us surrender the whole stronghold, lock, stock, and barrel. The gates have been flung open to the besiegers. Let them be easy in their minds. The traitor won't betray them. Now if too soon you yield, too soon you'll lose your love. Denials must be sometimes mingled with dalliance. You must sometimes keep your lover begging and praying and threatening before your door. Sweet things are bad for us. Bitters are the best tonic for the jaded appetite. More than one ship has sailed to perdition with a following wind. What makes men indifferent to their wives is that they can see them when they please. So shut your door and let your surly porter growl, "There's no admittance here!" This will renew the slumbering fires of love.

Now let us take the buttons off the foils, and to it with naked weapons, though, likely enough, I am instructing you for my own undoing. When you have netted your youthful novice, let him, at first, imagine he's the only one to enjoy your favours. But soon let him apprehend a rival. Let him think there's someone else with whom he has to share your charms. Some such tricks as these are needed, or his ardour would soon die down. A horse never runs so fast as when he has other horses to catch up and outpace. A slight gives a new life to our dying flame, and I confess that, for my own part, I couldn't go on loving unless I had a set-back to endure from time to time. But don't let him see so very much. Make him uneasy, and let him fear there's something more than just what meets his eye. Tell him that some imaginary servant always has his plaguey eye upon you. Tell him your husband's green with jealousy and always on the prowl. That will stimulate his ardour. A safe pleasure is a tame pleasure. Even if you were as free to have your fling as Thaïs, trump up some imaginary fears. When it would be easier for you to have him admitted by the door, insist on his climbing in at a window, and put on a scared expression when he looks at you. Then let some smart maid come rushing in crying, "We're ruined" and thrust him, trembling, into a cupboard. But sometimes let him have his pleasure of you undisturbed, lest he begin to ask himself whether the game is wholly worth the candle.

Let her body become a living letter.

I was not going to touch on the methods of hood winking a cunning husband and a watchful guard. A wife should fear her husband, she should be well looked after, that is quite as it should be, law, equity, decency—all require it so. But that you should have to put up with such servitude, you who have just been freed by the Lictor's rod that would be intolerable. Come to me, and I'll initiate you into the secret of giving them the slip. If you had as many warders as Argus had eyes, you shall, if you really are resolved, evade them all. For example, how is your warder going to hinder you from writing, during the time you're supposed to be in your bath? Is he going to prevent a servant who is in your secrets and aids you in your amours from carrying your missives in her bosom under a wide shawl? Couldn't she stuff them in her stocking, or hide them under the sole of her foot? But suppose your warder checkmates all these subterfuges, let your confidante make her shoulders your tablets, and let her body become a living letter. Characters written in fresh milk are a well-known means of secret communication. Touch them with a little powdered charcoal and you will read them. You may also do likewise with a stalk of green flax, and your tablets will, unsuspected, take the invisible imprint of what you write. Acrisius did everything he could think of to keep Danaë intact. Yet Danaë did what she should not have done, and made a grandsire of him. What can a woman's keeper do when there are so many theatres in Rome, when she can go sometimes to a chariot race, sometimes to religious celebrations where men are not allowed to show their faces? When the Bona Dea turns away from her temples all men save, perchance, a few whom she has bidden to come, when the unhappy keeper has to keep an eye on his mistress's clothes outside the baths, in which, maybe, men are securely hiding? And whenever she wants, some friend and accomplice will say she's sick, and for all her illness accommodate her with the loan of her bed. Then, tool the name of "adulterous" given to a duplicate key tells plainly enough the use to which we ought to put it. Nor is the door the only way to get into a woman's house. You can get the keeper under, however prying he may be, by giving him a good stiff drink, an even if you have to give him Spanish Wine, it's worth it. There are also potions that induce sleep and cloud the brain with a darkness as heavy as Lethean night. And your accomplice may usefully entice the pestilent fellow to hope for her favours, and by soft dalliance make him oblivious of the fleeting hours.

But why should I teach you these tedious and minute devices when the man may be bought for a trifling tip. Presents, believe me, seduce both men and gods. Jove himself is not above accepting a present. What will the wise man do, when a very fool knows the value of a gift? A present will even shut the husband's mouth. But only tip the keeper once a year. When he's held out his hand once, he'll be holding it out for ever. I lately complained, I remember, that one must beware of one's friends. That unwelcome statement was not addressed solely to men. If you are too confiding, others will win the quarry that belonged to you and someone else will net the hare that you had started. That very kind friend, who lends you her room and her bed, has more than once been on excessively friendly terms there with your lover. And don't have too pretty servant-maids about you either. More than one maid has played her mistress's part for me.

Oh, what a fool I am! Why do I let my tongue run away with

me like that? Why do I offer my naked bosom to be pierced? Why do I betray myself? The bird doesn't tell the fowler the way to snare her. The hind does not train the hounds to hunt her. No matter, if only I can be of service, I will loyally continue to impart my lessons, even if it means another Lemnian outrage. Act then, my dears, in such a way as to make us think you love us, there's nothing easier, for a man readily believes what he wants to believe. Look on a man seductively, keep sighing deeply, ask him why he's been so long in coming, make out you're jealous, sham indignation, look as if you're weeping, and even scratch his face for him. He'll very soon believe that you adore him, and as he looks upon your sufferings he'll exclaim, "The woman's simply mad about me!" especially if he's a coxcomb and thinks that even a goddess would fall in love with him. But if he doesn't run quite straight himself, don't, whatever you do, put yourself out too much about it. Don't go and lose your head if you hear that you are not the only pebble on the beach. And don't be in too much of a hurry to believe everything you hear. Think of Procris, and be warned by he, how dangerous it is to be too credulous.

Nigh the soft slopes of flowery Hymettus is a hallowed fount whose lips are fledged with tender green, and all around low-growing shrubs form not so much a wood, a woodland brake, there the 'arbutus offers a kindly shelter, rosemary and laurel and the dark-leaved myrtle shed their perfume far and wide-there likewise grow the thick-leaved box, the fragile tamarisk, the humble clover and the soaring pine. The leaves of all these divers trees and plants and the tips of the blades of grass, tremble in the breeze, set a-dance by the soft breath of the zephyrs. Hither young Cephalus, leaving his comrades and his dogs would often come to rest his limbs o'erwearied with the chase, and here, he oft would say, "Come, gentle Zephyr, steal into my breast and cool the heat wherewith I am opprest." It happened once some busybody heard him and must needs report these harmless words unto his anxious spouse. Procris no sooner heard this name of Zephyr than, deeming Zephyr was some rival, she was stricken dumb with grief and fell into a swoon. Pale was she, pale as those belated clusters which, when the wine-harvest is over, whiten at the first touch of frost, or like those ripe quinces which bend down the branches with their weight, or like the wild cherry ere yet it is ripe enough for our tables. As soon as she came to herself, she rent the flimsy garments that covered her bosom and scored her face with her nails. Then swift as lightning, in a tempest of fury, her hair flying in the wind, she tore across the country like some fierce Maenad. When she reached the fatal spot, she left her companions in the valley, and treading stealthily made her way boldly into the forest. What deed, O senseless Procris, dost thou meditate, hiding thyself thus? What fatal resolution arms thy distracted heart? Doubtless thou thinkest thou wilt see Zephyr, thine unknown rival, come upon the scene, thou thinkest with thine eyes to witness the unconscionable scene. Now dost thou repent thee of thy deed. For 'twere horror to surprise the guilty pair. Now dost thou glory in thy rashness. Love tortures thee and tosses thy bosom this way and that. All explains and excuses thy credulity. the place, the name, the story told thee, and that fatal gift that lovers have for believing that their fears are true. As soon as she saw the trampled grass and the print of recent footsteps, her heart beat faster than ever.

Already the noontide sun had curtailed the shadows and looked down at equal distances upon the East and West, when Cephalus, the son of the Cyllenian god, comes to the forest and bathes his face in the cool waters of a spring. Hidden close at hand, Procris, torn with suspense, gazes at him unseen. She sees him lie on the accustomed sward and hears him cry: "Come, thou sweet Zephyr, come thou cooling breeze." O what a joyful surprise is hers, she sees her error, and how a name had led her mind astray. Once more she is herself. Her wonted colour comes again, she rises to her feet and longs to fling herself into her husband's arms. But as she rises, she makes a rustling in the leaves. Cephalus, thinking it some wild creature of the woods, quickly seizes his bow, and even now he holds in his hands the fatal shaft. What, O hapless one, art thou about to do? 'Tis no wild animal... stay thy hand! Alas, it is too late, thy wife lies low, pierced by the arrow thou thyself hast sped! "Alas, alas," she cried. "Thou has stricken the breast of one who loved thee. And now that Zephyr, who did cause me so to err, bears away my spirit in the breeze. Ah me, I die... at least let thy beloved hand close my eyelids." Cephalus, distraught with grief, bears in his arms his dying loved one, and with his tears doth bathe her cruel wound.

Little by little the soul of rash Procris ebbs from her bosom, and Cephalus, his lips pressed close to hers, receives her during breath.

But let us pursue our voyage and, so that our wearied bark may reach the haven at last, let us have done with illustrations and speak straight to the point. No doubt you are expecting me to conduct you to banquets, and you would like me to tell you what I have to teach you thereupon. Don't come too soon, and don't show all your graces till the torches are alight. Venus likes delay, and waiting lends an added value to your charms. Even if you were plain, eyes dimmed by wine would think you beautiful, and night would fling a veil over your imperfections. Take the food with the tips of your fingers, and you must know that eating is itself an art. Take care to wipe your hand, and don't leave dirty finger-marks about your mouth. Don't eat before meals when you are at home, and when you are at table, learn to be moderate and to eat a little less than you feel inclined to. If the son of Priam had seen Helen eating like a glutton, he would have taken to hating her. "What a fool I was," he would have said, "to have carried off such a thing as that!" It were better for a young woman to drink, rather than to eat, too freely. Love and wine go very well together. However, don't drink more than your head will stand. Don't lose the use of your head and feet, and never see two things when only one is there. It's a horrible thing to see a woman really drunk. When she's in that state, she deserves to be had by the first comer. When once she's at table, a woman should not drop off to sleep. A sleeping woman is a whoreson temptation to a man to transgress the bounds of modesty.

I am ashamed to proceed, but Venus whispers encouragingly in my ear. "What you blush to tell," says she, "is the most important part of the whole matter." Let every woman, then, learn to know herself, and to enter upon love's battle in the pose best suited to her charms. If a woman has a lovely face, let her lie upon her back, if she prides herself upon her hips let her display them to the best advantage. Melanion bore Atalanta's legs upon his shoulders, if your legs are as beautiful as hers, put them in the same position. If you are short, let your lover be the steed. Andromache, who was as tall as an Amazon, never comported herself like that with Hector. A woman, who is conspicuously tall, should kneel with her head turned slightly sideways. If your thighs are still lovely with the charm of youth, if your bosom is without a flaw, lie aslant upon your couch, and think it not a shame to let your hair float unbraided about your shoulders. If the labours of Lucina have left their mark upon you, then, like the swift Parthian, turn your back to the fray. Love has a thousand postures, the simplest and the least fatiguing is to lie on your right side.

Never did the shrine of Phoebus Apollo, never did Jupiter Ammon, deliver surer oracles than the sayings chanted by my Muse. If the art which I so long have practised has aught of worth in it, then list to me, my words will not deceive you. So, then, my dear ones, feel the pleasure in the very marrow of your bones, share it fairly with your lover, say pleasant, naughty things the while. And if Nature has withheld from you the sensation of pleasure, then teach your lips to lie and say you feel it all. Unhappy is the woman who feels no answering thrill. But, if you have to pretend, don't betray yourself by over-acting. Let your movements and your eyes combine to deceive us and gasping, panting, complete the illusion. Alas that the temple of bliss should have its secrets and mysteries. A woman who after enjoying the delights of love, asks for payment from her lover, cannot surely but be joking. Don't let the light in your bedroom be too bright, there are many things about a woman that are best seen in the dimness of twilight. Now, there, I've done, my pleasant task is o'er. Unyoke, for surely 'tis high time, the swans that have been harnessed this long while unto my car. And now, my fair young pupils, do as your youthful lovers did awhile ago, upon your trophies write, "Ovid was our master."